MUSIC FOR A BROKEN PIANO

James Baker Hall

MUSIC FOR A
BROKEN PIANO

FICTION COLLECTIVE

NEW YORK

First edition
Copyright © 1982 James Baker Hall
All rights reserved.
ISBN 0-914590-79-0 pbk. ISBN 0-914590-78-2 cloth
LCCN: 82-084670

A section of this novel appeared, in an earlier form, in Chicago Review.

Published by Fiction Collective, c/o Flatiron Book Distributors, 175 Fifth Ave NYC 10010.

Typeset by Open Studio in Rhinebeck, N.Y., a non-profit facility for writers, artists and independent literary publishers, supported in part by grants from the New York State Council on the Arts and the National Endowment for the Arts.

for Barry Spacks

MUSIC FOR A BROKEN PIANO

When they weren't talking permanent community there around the fireplace in the big dining room, they were talking Makar. Some of the messages he pinned up on the bulletin board were straightforward enough, *U.C./ Long ago/ I declared WAR against arrogance & IGNORANCE,* or *A-2/ Note:/ please don't try to harm or even touch my BLACK MADONNA/ she will love & radiate/ the universe so dont/ be unkind to her,* or *They attacked mi (do ray mi)/ 25 miles from HOme/ with MENTAL, BIOLOGICAL, CHEMI-CAL warfare;* but others were a good deal more cryptic, *Win Yen/ I Won/ Long ago/ on the AGEAN SEE/ wind I wuz Sophocles/ so turn if you are not True;* and still others were flat-out incomprehensible to almost everyone there. Like everything that he did, or was imagined doing, his messages got scrutinized more or less closely by everyone, and even those who tried to dismiss them found that they had to dismiss them again and again.

Makar lived on the second floor of an old barn that had been converted into a dormitory and studios, in more of a stall than a room, four walls and a door but no ceiling; surrounded by young people, five males and two females, all like him without real privacy. He was the only man at Farmington without a woman, or the possibility of a woman—or so it seemed for the first half of the summer. Obvious as that was and important as it would seem, it was difficult for anyone to talk about, impossible except among close friends. It had the feel of some kind of racial slur, an effort to get a hold of him in some cheap, discredited way.

One of his trickier declarations was to masturbate each morning when he woke up, loudly. For the first few days the young people in the

Barn lay there in their beds and listened, incredulous and a little embarrassed—not only was he not trying to hide it, he was proclaiming it. Even though they prided themselves on being liberated, and even though each had every reason to believe that the others there in the Barn were hearing the same thing every morning, still it took them a while to talk to one another about it; and yet a while longer to tell anybody who did not live there. And even then it was a loaded subject, set about with kinks and backlashes. For one thing, they felt sorry for him; for another, they found it exciting, the way he carried on. It was enough for most, young and old alike, that he was black and crazy a lot of the time—too much that he insisted on being something special beyond all that. Not too many years before, or too many years later, circumstances would have been more congenial for a World Teacher —which was how he described himself on his application: Mathematician, Musician, Dancer, Poet and World Teacher. But in 1969 it was difficult, and at Farmington nearly impossible, especially among the young, for one person to sit comfortably at the feet of another, even a Black.

When he got off the bus from Detroit, dressed in full-length flowing red robes and carrying a brown corduroy drawstring bag that for weeks was a mystery, he was met with a smile by the Director of the community, Nathan, a big smile and a hand extended in greeting. And there they stood in the bus station, suspended amid the paperback racks and the fountain cokes and the weights on stacks of newspapers —a fat black lady with a shopping bag waddled past, showing the rolls of her stockings on the backs of her knees—suspended while Makar decided whether or not to shake Nathan's hand. Which he did, finally, jacking the world back down from its lean, a dime left on a stack of papers. Makar was a small man, no match for Nathan if it came to that —or so you would have thought—and no one saw him except at lunch and supper, often for days at a time. Soon he occupied, nonetheless, more space in the community than the other thirty-nine people taken together.

Around the fireplace, where plans were hatched and omelettes prepared, friendships made and unmade, you could always get the latest report on the local investments—something of a dormitory bull session, of a family conference, the history of the day, the week, the life. Although Makar never sat on a couch, where someone could sit next to him (nor would he ride in the back seat of a car), occasionally he joined what was happening there—and a group of three or four would double within minutes. Word got about that quickly, people dropped what they were doing and came. And others came wandering into Van Velder without having gotten the word, not knowing why they were coming, or thinking that they did, to meet someone or to play the piano or to help in the kitchen—only to find themselves drawn to the fireplace where Makar Atnui Aknada was ensconced in the over-stuffed chair. There were other times when he seemed to be making himself accessible, especially after meals when he stayed at the table drinking tea, but until he made a move toward the fireplace he had an inviolable space around him—something they had to learn the hard way.

Mealtime was when you associated with those you did not see otherwise; seldom did anyone sit with the same people at two meals running, or in the same place, especially early on in the summer. But Makar always sat in the same seat, at the head of the head table, facing the door. For the first few days he got to Van Velder ahead of everyone else and took that seat long before the food was served—even when he was supposed to be helping prepare the meal or set the tables. And there emphatically he sat, back straight, chin up, often with his eyes closed, one arm always stretched out on the table—until quickly enough everybody recognized his claim on that chair, even those who were not ready yet to honor it. The first two times that Makar did not show up early, Bobo sat himself down at the head of the head table, facing the door, half principle, half put-on (which seemed to characterize everything that he did). And Makar, stepping through the door into the sudden silence, turned on his heel both times and vanished, going without supper. Much argument ensued, the upshot of which was: for the rest of the summer either Makar sat there or no one did.

Eating at the head table was for many like hosting a visiting celebrity without knowing what he was famous for. Sometimes Makar waited on himself, sometimes he permitted others to wait on him, but he never waited on anybody else. He conducted his meal with great dignity, slowly and gracefully, every move at once practical and ritualistic, enjoying the food and himself with an intensity that changed everything around him. You could refuse to pay attention to him, but you could not escape an awareness of him—which in turn was a new awareness of yourself. He made you feel, if nothing else, that you were sloppy and distracted at your food. Obvious as he made it that he did not want to talk, he was always polite when spoken to, at first anyway, and he would answer whatever was asked of him, after his fashion. When the meal was finished and he stayed on with a cup of tea, his chair turned sideways, one arm stretched out on the table, and when he remained there long after the surfaces were cleared and the floor swept and the chairs returned to their places, often with a look of great satisfaction on his face—it was hard to believe that he was not finally accessible. He was still as remote as when he was wrapped in his robes in a bar ditch miles away, but it took Nathan's assumption to the contrary one evening early in the summer to get that established conclusively.

Against his wife's advice, Nathan got up the nerve and went over and sat down next to Makar, turning his chair out, crossing his legs, laying his brown muscular arm on the table next to Makar's.

"How's it going?" he said.

"Pretty fair for a square," Makar said.

There was a pause. They were looking at one another, both of them smiling.

"Where were you today? I didn't see you around."

"I was around, I reckon," Makar said. "If what you mean is Around. Ain't no other place to be, I reckon. Is that what you mean?"

"I was just making conversation," Nathan said.

Makar chuckled.

Nathan suspected him of being doped out of his head—which presented a special problem to him, just as the color of his skin did.

They had not taken their eyes off one another.

Around Makar's neck, on a thin leather strap, was a charm of some sort, a hand-carved wooden charm—Nathan pointed to it and asked him what it was.

Without taking his eyes off the white man, Makar lifted his hand from his teacup—Nathan thought it was going to the charm, oh this, it's.... But it did not. His black hand turned Nathan's pointing finger away, turned it away without even touching it.

"I don't understand," Nathan said.

"Please," was all Makar said.

"Please what? Did I offend you somehow?"

"Did I come up and sit down and cross my legs?"

"Do you want me to leave?"

"I thought you was just making conversation."

"I was!"

"Then how come you start shooting arrows into my heart?"

"I was just asking about your thing there!"

"If you're going to go shooting arrows into my heart, you got to be Cupid, you know what I mean?"

"I wasn't shooting *arrows* into your heart. Come on now!"

"You was just asking about 'my thing'," Makar said, with just the barest trace of mockery.

"I was just asking about.... " He started to point again, but he caught himself.

"You was just talking about my thing, and I was just talking about your thing—I suppose you'd say we was just making conversation, is that what you'd say?"

Nathan took a deep breath. "I just meant.... "

Makar interrupted him, his voice bearing down, becoming clipped now. "If you're Cupid, that's one thing, but you're not Cupid, are you? I mean if you're Cupid now, that's all right, you can go around shooting arrows, but I suspect you're just Nathan, you know what I mean? Your name's Nathan, ain't it?"

Several people were gathered around now, listening. He'd certainly been thinking that he knew who he was, and acting like it—too many times each day for too long now. My name is Nathan, he had said, over and over and over, oblivious to what he was saying until he said it at least one time too many—to Toni McHugh, the new woman. She was there watching now, a great smile on her face, one hand in her hip pocket, the other holding a hammer—as though Makar weren't enough. Nathan was beginning to sweat. He had the feeling that she was somehow as much a part of what was going on as he and Makar were—though he had not the slightest idea who had made it that way or how it could be so.

She and her husband were two of the eight people who were being paid to be there, a core community as he had thought of it, guaranteeing the presence of enough older people—which included Makar, something that only Nathan and his wife Meriwether knew. Toni McHugh and Warren Medders had showed up only yesterday, ten days late. They hadn't even called to tell him what was going on. They were the only people Nathan had sought out and asked to apply— something he vowed never to do again. In an old VW bus replete with flower decals they had pulled slowly up the driveway just after dinner, as the volleyball game was getting under way, and stopped in front of Van Velder. She had long blond hair. A neatly folded red bandana was tied around her forehead, and above that: sunglasses, cocked in a way that was more tired than sexy. It was not uncommon for such a van to pull in there or up at Franklin to check the place out, but everyone seemed to know immediately who it was. The volleyball game stopped. Toni turned off the motor. Everyone converged on the van to greet them—except Nathan. He was left standing alone on the court with the ball in his hands, angry—not only at their arrogance past and present but at his own impotence before it. From the sidelines, with their three-year-old child in one arm, Meriwether ruefully extended the other for the ball—mimicking the overworked woman wifing the put-upon man. He was probably not the only one there who wanted to withhold such a welcome, but he was surely the one person who was not free to do it—or so he believed. With a wry shrug he pitched the ball to his wife, something Hebraic in his figure, the large bearded sternness, the resignation; hooking his thumbs in the pockets of his jeans, he shrugged again, thinking that it probably served him right. He had imagined this scene taking place in the privacy of his office, where they had come to introduce themselves and explain their behavior; he had planned to listen patiently to their apology and then to tell them exactly what he thought of it. If he was a fool, playing the administrator to every compromise that presented itself, right there in the middle of a war on arrogance and ignorance at that, he reckoned he had the comfort at least of a lot of company, a whole community of clowns, including now yet another head of long blond hair, yet another show of doves and flowers. As he walked toward the van he knew what costume Toni McHugh would be wearing; her husband would have a beard and a Republican father; the book box in the back end of the old VW would contain worn copies of the *Whole Earth Catalogue* and Alan Watts' *What Is Zen*. He knew too, in trying to drop his quarrel with them, the possibility of a true welcome, transforming a bad start into a good one. When he had to reach through and over the press of people, he wasn't thinking how ludicrous this all was but how wholesome—just as he had when he walked across the bus station smiling, his large hand out to Makar. Loud and clear he said who he was, as always.

She put her fist in his hand, her tiny fist, her thin wrist—and smiled. The strangest thing about that strange handshake was its intimacy. She did not say who she was. She did not say anything.

o o o

Music for a Broken Piano

She had large blue-grey eyes that looked straight at you without blinking. She looked directly at whoever was talking whether she was being talked to or not, and when you turned your eyes away she watched your lips. Her stare was too open to be challenging, too attentive. Her bleached hair was growing out dark at the roots, but there was nothing hard looking about her, certainly nothing tacky. Her hair, teased up by the bandana, appeared to have jumped up and away from her dark head, brightening dramatically. A cat in her lap was stretching its legs up her chest, working its claws in the sweatshirt between her breasts, rubbing the top of its head under her chin. Another cat was lying full-length at her shoulder, along the back of the seat, its eyes closed. In all the lists of her praise and credits no one had mentioned how good looking she was—because, Nathan saw immediately, she would not have approved. His impression was of someone who had never thought of explaining herself, to anyone. Behind her a large black Labrador was going from window to smudged-up window barking loudly at the resident pets, who (if they hadn't already left) were keeping a distance.

Nathan was willing to believe now that she hadn't spoken because there was too much noise, that she had turned off the motor and sat there waiting not for yet more special treatment but for the animals to get used to one another.

Nothing was said about their being late, not then, not later. What they talked about was the projection room, which in his effort to lure her there he had promised. When he told her it wasn't ready, she winced—but she never stopped smiling.

He apologized—and wished immediately he hadn't.

He did not want anyone overhearing that absurd conversation he had with Makar the next night at the table, especially not Toni McHugh. And there with her hammer she stood, her frank eyes going back and forth as though she were watching a tennis match—a look of great amusement on her face.

"You're not Cupid, are you?"

Nathan took a deep breath and there issued forth from his learned mouth what must have been Western civilization's longest, whitest, least defensive defense of finger pointing. He was facing everything out, treating Makar just as he would treat anybody else—which was more than he had been able to do yet, more in fact than anybody had been able to do. He was pleased with himself, and the people who were listening were impressed, most of them anyway. They were convinced, or at least hopeful, that patience and good intentions and reasonableness would prevail. But things went from bad to worse. The more patient and well-intentioned and reasonable Nathan became, the more impatient and arrogant and rude and cryptic Makar was—until finally he made an obscure gesture over his teacup and told Nathan to shut up and quit apologizing.

It was not the first time that day they had encountered one another, though Nathan did not know that. Early that morning, as it was getting light, Makar appeared in the bushes outside the window of Nathan's office up the hill and watched him do push-ups. Nathan got up before dawn each morning, carrying his shoes downstairs so as not to awaken Meriwether and the child; after listening to the news on a small green transistor radio that he kept always at hand he ran three miles, exactly three, and then did sit-ups and push-ups on the floor of the office before sitting down at the desk or going into the darkroom to work. Watching him do push-ups was to have their difficulty flatly denied: he could do fifty in a set without a pause, as strong at the end as at the beginning, snapping them off, his powerful body as straight as an illustration. Makar was wearing a peaked cap, the kind that Robin Hood is pictured wearing, a red peaked cap and a mid-length brocade cape. He appeared suddenly in the bushes outside the window and stared in, close up, bold, nothing apologetic about him at all, he was right there at the window looking in, watching Nathan snap off the push-ups as though there were no effort involved. He was thinking where and how he would hit this powerful man if he ever had to, and how he would kill him if it came to that. Nathan was no threat to him, it was just a habit of his mind, one of the ways he sorted things out. As far as Nathan knew he was the only one up at Farmington, and for that matter he may have been right. Everyone else, including the black man standing there at the window, may have been still asleep in their beds or in a culvert miles away. When Nathan was done with his exercises he stood up and turned to the window, and, combing his full handsome beard with his hands, stared out dreamily at the coming light. Makar was there in the bushes only a few yards away, standing stock still with a look on his face and staring back at him—but Nathan did not see him. It was as though the man was not there. Perhaps there was some ordinary explanation, reflections or a blind spot, or perhaps it was a really intense instance of the sort of thing that Nathan experienced later that same day when Makar told him to shut up and quit apologizing. It was all he could do then to look at the man, impossible for him to see much of anything.

"What are you talking about?" Nathan said calmly. "I'm not apologizing!"

And he wasn't: he clearly wasn't: his tone throughout had been firm, impressively respectful of them both, nothing ingratiating or apologetic about it. But the crazy thing was, by then everybody wanted him to shut up and quite apologizing. He even felt that way himself.

Everybody except Toni, who seemed merely amused.

The day had been crazy with apologizing and not apologizing.

From the morning exercises he had gone into the darkroom, two hours with his own work before breakfast; he had just looked at the clock to see how much more time he had left. He could not have been more surprised had Makar knocked on the darkroom door, or more pleased. He thought she had come to explain and apologize, or otherwise mend fences. Pleased, but cautious—if for no other reason, the projection room still had to be dealt with. He was wary of her, and soon he knew why.

He had no idea what she was doing there.

The thoroughness with which she examined the prints he was making had the same effect as glancing through them, suggested that she was looking for something that simply was not there. When she was done she said nothing. The condescension did not surprise him, but her lack of subtlety did. He thought he knew for sure now who she was.

She was looking straight at him.

She had several different smiles, each of them a different face, but her eyes were always the same lidless thing. He could look straight at it, but he couldn't focus. She was sitting on the edge of the sink, her feet off the floor, her hands at her sides for balance. He could see the outline of her panties under her faded jeans, curving tightly over the thigh. With looks like hers you could act that way and get by with it, he supposed—lay it all at the feet of male chauvinism. She was the reason he had chosen married life, and kept on choosing it.

"I don't like the way you looked at those pictures," he said.

She blushed. He saw it hit her inside before it surfaced—first in her eyes, around her eyes, a shock. They weren't always the same at all. They closed, the lids blushing.

"You're right," she said. She reached out and put her hand on the back of his—which was propped up on the sink, holding a towel. "You're absolutely right. I don't like it either."

It was less an apology than a statement of fact. He saw again now what he had seen with her tiny fist in his hand the night before, her thin wrist—she didn't traffic in explanations, hers or anybody else's. She had come, she told him, to find out where certain things were. She wasn't expecting him to build the projection room for her—she didn't even want him to leave his own work long enough to show her how to proceed on her own.

"Just tell me where the tools are," she said.

The hammer was right there—he handed it to her.

Hard as it was for him to believe that she knew her way around already, he became convinced, the longer he talked to her, that she probably did, more than well enough to find everything she needed. Already she knew by name many of the people there, and in some instances she knew a remarkable lot more.

Stung by Makar's accusation that night he felt in her frank eyes, in the amusement with which she held the hammer, that already she knew more than he did.

"You're not Cupid, are you?"

He had the feeling that she understood better than he did what that was supposed to mean.

"Then shut up," Makar told him, "and quit apologizing."

Toni laughed, tossing the big hammer from one hand to the other—and, as though she had seen enough, left.

When it was over he got bragged on for the way he had handled himself, refusing to be irritated or intimidated—everybody wanted to be proud of him, and was—even Meriwether, who was finding it hard these days to be anything but angry. Even Nathan himself felt that way, no trace of apology in him, if not proud then at the very least quite satisfied. Mulling the episode over later that night and the next day, he had only one qualm—what had Toni McHugh been thinking? He came to the conclusion that he would never know, probably was not meant to—that in fact he didn't particularly want to know what was going on in her pretty but arrogant head.

When Makar joined others around the fireplace, however, he was making himself accessible—though very much on his own terms at first, resulting in protracted negotiations. The young people, especially, wanted to trade what it was like to be them for what it was like to be him. But Makar wouldn't trade. He would World Teacher them, but he didn't want anything to do with the rub tub, or with getting into anybody's head, or letting anybody get into his—nothing to do with any of that, and the tension mounted. "If he doesn't want to be part of the community"—you heard this all the time—"what's he doing here?" One theory was, he was the advance reconnaissance for a whole army of black berets who would descend on Farmington some-day soon and burn the place down. Another was that he was hiding out from the laws of three states, or a dozen. Another that he spent nine months a year kissing white ass for a living, and Farmington was the balance of nature. What brought him to the fireplace (aside from dope—which he could have gotten easily enough if he wanted without having to sit there to smoke it) was something of a mystery. Some said that it was the flattery, what man would not have been drawn to all that attention. Others that he could not have cared less, if there were anyone in the world unaffected by what others thought of him it was Makar. Certainly that was borne out in the fact that there was no correlation whatsoever between the amount or the kind of attention he got there and the frequency with which he came or the length of time that he stayed or how he acted when he was there. He could be more or less agreeable or disagreeable, but it never had anything to do with what was going on in the rest of the world, not as far as anybody at Farmington could tell anyway. Joe Lainard and Alan Sinclair, both much respected, were already convinced that Makar was some kind of genius, and Nathan himself was often inclined to agree. Phyllis Brodsky, a psychiatrist and poet, thought that he was insane, that the only question was whether or not he was dangerous. But most could not make up their minds. The older people kept their distance and settled for casual conversation, but a lot of the young were determined to get up front with him—which meant that he had to be there with them.

They were at it now, Bobo and Jerry and Rafe and Loraine and Rhonda: they told their hearts' truths at Makar, only to get World Taught, at best, and from the moon at that, long slow sliding elliptical obscurantisms. Tonight the big thing was the Panthers, they wanted to know what Makar thought about the Panthers. He smiled and sipped his tea and chuckled. "Out of sight," he said, "out of sight." And then chuckled. His laugh came from way back in the corner of his mouth, a kind of rasping caw, a Donald Duck cross between a crow and one of those hook-shaped spit suckers that dentists put in your mouth: the vocalization of his smile was what it was, mocking if you wanted it to be, maybe even if you didn't, impossible to pin down: it spun, right along with the rest of him: a series of liquid explosions, raspy, each one coming on a little quicker than the one before, but not quite rhythmical either. Out of sight, he said, and what at first sounded like a formula didn't the more you thought about it. He then went on to talk, approvingly you realized some time later, about Robert E. Lee. Nobody wanted to be stupid, or honky, they were all running helter-skelter from the suburbs, the whole work-a-day commonsense Kansas head was suspect, no dude was going to get caught *there*. So he got the benefit of the doubt, Makar did, always. When they asked him what he thought about Bobby Seale or John F. Kennedy or Kwame Nkrumah or Baba Ram Dass or numerology or astrology or the third world or the SDS, what they heard the first far-out time around was that he didn't think at all, had given it up a long time ago as a lost cause (if, some would have said, it was ever his to give up). But then they got to mulling it over and they weren't so sure. Everybody was wary of being put on, especially the grownups, but wary also of being simple-minded, especially the young, and they were all forever dealing with the fact that common sense could make just as much a fool of you as a Hollywood Hindu. There is a story about Robert Oppenheimer, told by a friend, how he and his colleagues would be sitting around the room talking, following with great concentration the logic of some proposition, into which Oppenheimer would drop a seemingly irrelevant remark. It would give them all pause, since it was Robert Oppenheimer who made it—often an embarrassed pause, for it seemed to reveal his inattention to what was being said. Then later on in the discussion, when they finally reached the point that he had made, they would discover that instead of being out of it he was just that far ahead. Shortly after the community convened in early June, *The New York Times Sunday Magazine* carried an article in which the most famous Black poet in the country said that there were only three Afro-American artists who had not sold out, among them Joseph Mana—which was one of Makar's aliases. That raised the stakes around the fireplace a quantum, enhancing the cause of those who were able and inclined to see Makar as a kind of Oppenheimer. Somewhere on the other side of the obvious irrelevance of his remarks was the tease of some deeper thought; you would begin to wonder whether there was not some connection after all between the Panthers and Robert E. Lee, maybe even a profound one; and you were a little less inclined the next time, perhaps, to assume that Makar was as mindless as he at times seemed. Not that it made an iota of practical difference what you thought or how you treated him, Oppenheimer or fool, genius or con man or spaced-out nigger; he smiled at all assumptions alike and just laughed, that weird spit-sucking caw from the back corner of his mouth: he went right on being obscure and inaccessible to his fans and his detractors alike. Although it was common knowledge that Makar read *The Sunday New York Times* front to back every week on Wednesday afternoon in the living room at Franklin House, no one ever mentioned that much-discussed article to him, or even knew for sure whether or not he had seen it. It meant something special to them, and no one wanted to deal with his indifference to it. They were beginning to understand—though no one could have articulated it yet—that it would take more than America's most famous Black poet to make what was in *The New York Times* real to Makar. And more than respect for Joseph Mana to make America's most famous Black poet real.

After weeks of pussy-footing around the fireplace, Bobo came up with a new move, a deeper connection than had been made to date. He threw the peace sign at Makar: held it out at arm's length and pumped it at him several quick times, saying "Cryptic! Cryptic!" For weeks now they had all been sitting around in various defensive modes of white finger-pointing, asking him what he thought about everything they thought about, and then attending to his responses as though he credited the question, lived in the very same world they did, Farmington, Massachusetts, summer, 1969, the United States of America, a ratty bunch of thirty-nine more or less independent states of being in pilgrimage to some Delphi, their wide eyes stuck down the black hole of this crazy nigger's mouth, listening to spit suck and crow caw for the voice of the oracle. In other words they had been respectful, each after his fashion of that place and time, generous and kind and loving and open and *respectful* every one. And then Bobo came up with his new number: it weren't respectful at all: it was downright impudent in fact. He threw the peace sign at the head of the head table himself, comically stiff-armed him with it five or six quick times, saying "Cryptic! Cryptic!" Impudent, and a little bit scary. There was violence in that arm pumping out at Makar, telling him to go piss up a Hindu rope: in the partial fist pumping close to Makar's nose there was something of a threat being shaken in the black man's face.

"Cryptic! Cryptic!" Bobo said.

It took everybody by surprise. Nathan was there, and when he got over the jar of it his appreciation of Bobo soared—which was a relief to him. Bobo, his former student, represented all manner of problems to Nathan. For one thing Nathan was responsible for Bobo getting busted, something that Bobo did not know, would not have suspected even in his worst ideas of Nathan. And for another he was out of a mental institution under Nathan's custody. They had come to that moment from bad times, he and Bobo, and they were headed for worse. So Nathan's relief was deep—he would have liked nothing better than to see this brash young man triumph. He was convinced that if a balance of power were possible, without which nothing useful could happen between Makar and the rest of them—just old child-hood roles played over and over again—it would be struck just this way, out of the cryptic mold of a new tone.

It even took Makar by surprise. He was not smiling. He was staring at Bobo, but he was not smiling, and he was not spinning that liquid laugh out of the back corner of his mouth. He was not on the moon at all for a change, but under a dream he was having, right there at the fireplace: staring at Bobo, his great bulging eyes locked on the cryptic smirk. He was stuck there, dealing piddly-shit with a bunch of hippies, a game of ups. Everybody was watching him, waiting for his response. When it came it was in the form of a white man's voice. *You're right, of course,* it said. *This charade is tiresome. You have no idea how tiresome, really. Had I one whit of honesty or decency, I would not burden you with it. I'm sorry. We're all sorry, I'm sure. For whatever that is worth.* Those who did not get the words got the change: they saw his face change, his whole presence change. He stood up, and shook his head vigorously, once, like a wet dog—shook something off. No one had any idea what had happened, but they all knew that something had: wherever they were a minute ago they were not there any longer. Without a trace of irony Makar bowed slightly from the waist to Bobo, then to Nathan, then to the others. And turned around and walked out, leaving them all bewildered.

When he was out of sight of Van Velder, Makar started to run. He crossed an open field and entered the woods and ran for more than a mile along a ridge, then turned downhill, his stride lengthening, and followed a stone fence to a creek that ran parallel to the highway into Northampton. At the creek he rested for a while, tying his shoes together and looping them over his belt at the small of his back. And then continued, at a quickened pace, for another mile and a half along the creek bank. He spent the night wrapped in his robes in a culvert several miles from Farmington.

At dawn, curled up in the warmth of his own body, he received a long distance person-to-person call for Joseph Mana, and when he heard the operators talking to one another, saying that they had their party now, he knew where the call was coming from: NASA, in Cocoa Beach. He was asked by a man he recognized to confirm his identity, which he did by using his white man's voice; and then he was asked to hold. It was only then that he knew that something big was up: Cocoa Beach was not the connection, it was the way the connection was being made: he heard the call being transferred, and he knew what he was hearing: no voices, just circuits opening and closing, and he knew that the call was going home, that one of three voices would be at the other end. He took a deep breath and shut his eyes and waited. It seemed to him that much of his life had been spent right there, breathing himself down, into a poise, waiting. He knew what he had to do and he knew how to do it, but still those circuits worked their ways on him, opening and closing down the empty corridors of his fear.

"Is that you?" the voice said.

"Depends on what you mean," Makar said.

"How are you?"

"Pretty fair for a square," he said.

"I'm happy to hear that. We got something we want you to do."

"I'm out," he said.

"Are you sure?"

"I'm out."

"You know I wouldn't be asking you if it weren't important. You're the only one.... You know what I mean. You could get there quick enough. You know what to do. It's pretty important."

"I'm out."

There was a silence at the other end.

Then, "How far out?"

There was another silence.

Makar said nothing.

"Where you living now?"

"On the moon," Makar said. "Is that far enough out?"

"Somebody was saying the other day they thought you were... unreliable. Is that the word?"

"Un-huh, un-huh. They say unreliable, huh? And you asking me if that's the word?"

"Well...you know what I mean."

"Un-huh. You mean *she* said that. Is that what you're trying to say?"

A long silence.

"Snake," Makar said.

"You know Snake?"

"Bettern you do, sounds like."

"Okay. She said you were on the other side."

"Other side of the moon maybe. From where I'm living there ain't no other side, you know what I mean? I'm out."

"I been hearing you were on the other side all along."

"I'll bet you hear a lot of shit like that, all the time."

"You sure you won't do it? This is the last time, I assure you. We'll make it worth your while."

"I'm out."

"Okay. When you're out, you're out. You always played straight with us, we'll always play straight with you. You don't have to worry about that."

I wasn't—till you mentioned it, Makar tried to say. But he'd lost his voice.

It was then that he knew that the circuit was dead, opening up again on the one sound.

And he realized that he was still on hold—the call was yet to go through. That's where he was living. He was not the only one. Other people had lost their voices too. There was nothing to do, but he could not do it yet.

On the way home, along a ridge and then past Diana's pool, he disappeared into a song—many people all at once, playing. He took his place, answering to no one. The law there was music—even the leader followed it—backwards, until you no longer knew where you were, or when.

It was then that a snake hit him, dropping him out.

Slithering across the ground, into the music, he became himself, writhing in pain.

That was it.

When he got back to Farmington the next day he rubbed his feet with olive oil, and after lunch pinned a note on the bulletin board: tracing the peace sign back to Churchill's V for Victory.

She was known those first few days as "the Driver," not because she had slaves and drove them but because with her that was not necessary. All Toni McHugh had to drive, it seemed, was nails. She didn't have to ask for help, she didn't even have to tell them what to do. Picking up a utility knife and a hammer she had only, it would seem, to keep her mind on what needed to be done. Watching her work, three or four strokes to the ten penny, you would find yourself watching more and more closely, and soon without a word being spoken you would find yourself holding whatever it was she would need next, waiting for the right moment to hand it to her. First Rafe, then Bobo and Rhonda and Jerry, they worked straight through both nights, sleeping a few hours in the afternoon, working sometimes in shifts, sometimes all together. The projection room took shape around the new woman like something in an animated film. In forty-eight hours it was done—one whole end of the Barn was tight, even in the daytime. More got done in the first two days Toni McHugh was there than in the two weeks previous. Even Meriwether helped them, the first time that she had joined in. Even Nathan had to admit that Toni was—in some ways at least—a model for the whole community. Late in the afternoon of the third day her people rounded up all the extra mattresses and delivered them, the McHugh-Medders van backed up to the door. That night the projection room opened, a screening of whatever whoever wanted to show, three gallons of wine and music afterwards, Crosby, Stills and Nash, the Moody Blues, Creedence. And the next night she got down to business.

Toni had come as a filmmaker, more highly recommended than anyone there (including her husband, who was said by everyone at

Yale to be the most gifted composer through there in years); but she was working now with slides, often in multiple projections. You lay on the floor, on your own mattress. For the first twenty or thirty minutes all you could see in the tall dark room was this one bright image, the Rancheros de Taos Church, and ten or twelve bodies stretched out on the floor there in front of it—the sculptured abode facade in a low flat light, the scale gone, as if subtle browns and greys and pinks had modeled themselves into shapes. All you could hear was the whirr of the projector. Sometimes you didn't hear even that. Once when Meriwether was there the big lab Nietzsche got up from his place in the corner and walked up and down the rows as though he were conducting an inspection, stopping in front of her to stare, first at her—it was the first time in she couldn't remember how long that she'd been looked at as something other than a housewife, a mother—then at the bright church projected on the wall. The Rancheros de Taos was replaced by images of cells, of light on water, of blood, of parts of cells, you were wrapped around with pulsing colors, recurring shapes and motions overlapping, the moons of Jupiter. Toni directed your attention from one part of your body to the next, telling you to hold it there, to relax into the tension. There were nights when Meriwether had very little idea how much time had passed. Suddenly she would become aware of the silence. It was as though Toni talked so that she could stop, cutting you loose. How strange it all was, how familiar! The projector whirred until it cooled out, then the room was perfectly still. The last fifteen minutes was whatever you did with that silence. For Meriwether it was the privacy she hadn't even known she wanted.

Meriwether didn't want to talk about it, especially not with Nathan —it was the kind of thing that brought out a special alertness in him, a wariness, as though he were listening for something in particular, waiting for you to let it slip out—but he was there on their bed when she got back from her first session, waiting to hear. Despite her efforts to be scrupulous and thorough she ended up, as she so often did, feeling as though she were hiding something, if not from him then from herself—angry, and not knowing why.

"What happens after you leave?" he asked.

"I come home, like a good little girl."

"I mean down there."

"I know what you mean."

"It's just a question."

"It is *not*."

"How come you're so defensive?"

"For the same reason you're so judgmental. Don't ask me where I've been, and then tell me I don't know what I'm talking about. It's not what you think it is, Nathan. She's a serious person."

"I didn't say she wasn't serious."

Propped up against the head board, his hairy chest and face in shadow, he was stretched out on top of the sheets in his pajama bottoms, the legs pulled up over his knees. A paperback rested on his crotch like a codpiece. His large perfectly formed feet conducted a steady life of their own: figure eights, over and over, the big toes touching each time in the center. Nothing else about him moved—his attention was fixed, absolutely, on her.

"Look, sweetie, I want you to go down there, or wherever you want to go. It'll be good for you. It'll be good for our marriage."

"If I go down there, it'll be because I *want* to, not because it's *good* for me, or *good* for our marriage."

"You know what I mean."

"Indeed I do. Exactly."

"Just tell me what you're so upset about."

She sat down on the bed and took hold of his feet, one in each hand, and held them—that's what she was upset about. He was always rowing a boat, but he never seemed to be in it.

"You've been encouraging me to get involved ever since we got here. Since before we came."

When she let them loose, his feet started up again.

"That's exactly what I just got through saying," he said.

This time she grabbed them, letting out a scream.

They both laughed.

"Then get off my back. Get off Toni's back."

"I wasn't aware that I was on her back."

"I'm going to tell you this about three thousand more times, and then that's going to be it. You're impossible. Absolutely impossible. Do you know that? I don't *know* what happens after I leave. I don't *care*. It's none of my *business*."

"Okay. Okay."

"I mean do you want to talk about it or don't you?"

"I want to talk about it, of course I want to talk about it."

"On the assumption that I've been down there and know, or that you haven't and know better? If you want me to have friends of my

own, then let me have friends of my own. Don't ask me to come back
and check it all out with you."

"You're right," he said. "You're absolutely right."

A similar exchange took place the next time she came back from the
projection room. She was as confused as he was by how angry she got
these days, and how often, and she too was a little frightened by it—
but for a change she wasn't depressed. She could imagine having her
own questions about Toni, given the chance, but for sure they
wouldn't be his—she was determined to break free.

"You think it's the rub tub and the dope den all rolled into one, and I
get the feeling you're going to go right on thinking it, no matter *what* I
say. How do you think it makes me feel to have to deal with your
suspicions all the time? She's the best thing that's happened to this
place—you've said as much yourself. Maybe they smoke before I get
there and while I'm there. Maybe they screw like alley cats—I don't
know. I don't *care*. That's *not* what I'm going down there for. I'm *not*
going to get VD lying on a mattress. I would appreciate a little of that
freedom you're always saying I've got."

"It's yours."

"You're damn right it is. And it's not yours to bestow on me."

"I didn't say I thought it was the rub tub and the dope den."

"You don't *have* to say it, Nathan. That's what I'm trying to tell
you. Don't you think I *know* what you're thinking? For christsakes I
think it *myself* a lot of the time. That, as they say, is the *problem*."

"What else do I think?"

"You want to know what's going on between Toni and Rafe."

"Don't tell me you don't."

"I didn't say that."

"What *is* going on?"

"I haven't the slightest idea."

"You never see one any more without the other."

"What's the matter with that?"

"Now *you* come off it."

"No. I'm serious."

"I didn't say anything was the matter."

She slapped his foot, hard. And then the other one.

He wiggled his toes at her, all at once.

"You're absolutely impossible," she said.

"I was merely registering the fact that she happens to be married to
someone else."

"And that she's been here only a short period of time."

"Well by god it's true."

"Are we going to go on and on like this? Forever?"

"Let's make a truce," he said. "We just won't talk about it."

"It's a deal. Not until we can do better than this."

That's where they left it. They had to leave it there several more times, but finally it stayed, off limits.

As Meriwether was befriending Toni, Nathan turned to her husband, sitting with him at meals, attending his lectures on John Cage, talking with him whenever the chance presented itself, listening to him talk to others. He saw in Medders an attractive young Robert McNamara with long hair and a beard, the same rimless glasses, the same compact body, the same kind of orderly well-informed mind, the same kind of attention and patience and concern for detail. In his late twenties he had about him already something of the elder statesman, the habits of a man long accustomed to being deferred to. You had to wonder how Toni McHugh responded to that. His eyes were a bright emphatic blue, and in profile, which was a trace Byronic, Medders was at times handsome, despite fifteen extra pounds around the waist and hips, twenty; but he slept ten and twelve hours a day and seemed to be avoiding his work—hints, Nathan thought, of something wrong. Attentive as he was to further evidence, however, he saw no weakness in the man. There was certainly nothing flabby about his politics—he was ready to give up his job to live at Farmington year round, which was a lot more than Nathan was willing to do. And there was certainly nothing evasive in the way he responded to you. One day after lunch he led Nathan outside by the wrist.

"You think I need somebody to talk to, don't you?"

It took Nathan by surprise. "Is there anything the matter with that? Don't most of us?"

"You're treating me like a cuckold."

Nathan blushed. "I certainly don't mean to be."

"There's nothing to talk about."

Nathan made a neither-this-nor-that gesture with his left hand, discarding something but without conviction.

"You don't believe that, do you?"

"No. I don't."

"One of us is wrong," Medders said.

"I might not be the right person to talk to. You might not want to talk.... "

"But you don't believe there's nothing to talk about."

He had the kind of eyes that repeated everything he said, even more clearly now, the challenge. "No," Nathan said. "I'm sorry. I do not." "I'll tell you something else you won't believe. She hasn't even fucked him yet. That's not what's going on."
"What is going on?"
"I don't make it my business."
"Do you approve?"
"I'm not in a position to approve or disapprove. And I don't ever intend to be."
"Let's drop it," Nathan said. "I'm sorry if I meddled."

Whatever was going on, Nathan did not trust it. He was willing to believe that he did not know what was up with the projection room, but not that nothing was. Soon enough his suspicions were vindicated, to his satisfaction anyway. A small community formed within the larger one, a group that stayed up all night and slept all day, hassling the rest of them about the three-meals-a-day kitchen. The basic schedule, they said, was left-over establishment bullshit, interfering with their way of life. Not that Toni said it, or anything else for that matter, ever—she acted as though the rest of the community didn't exist, except when it appeared at her door—it was her flunkies, Rafe and Bobo.
"Forget it," Nathan told them.
"I thought this was supposed to be a self-structuring community," Rafe said.
"Maybe next year," Nathan said.
"Can I quote you?"
"No."
"Can I?" Bobo said, cupping his genitals at the professor.
Nathan always had a hard time looking at him—distressed for having had Bobo busted, and for keeping it a secret, he knew at the same time he'd done what he had to. "You will anyway," Nathan told him.
"Is that permission?"
"No."
"No?!" Bobo stalked off, spun around and stalked back, in the role now of a cop who had just gotten to the scene. "Who is this kid? Is this the motherfucker giving you all the trouble?" He shoved Rafe face up against the wall and frisked him. He grabbed Nathan's camera off the desk, pretending to take a mug shot of him. "You know what you look

like, boy?" he said in Nathan's Memphis accent. "You look like the *Mafia!*"

He had to believe that at some level Bobo knew.

It was true, Rafe did look like the Mafia. With his shirt open, the tails tied over his navel, a kerchief around his neck and a cigarette hanging off his lip, Rafe was playing the South Boston street corner now in Bobo's skit. A small wiry Italian in his mid-twenties, he looked as though, given a suit and haircut and sunglasses, he would chauffeur the limo. In every respect he was as unlike Toni McHugh as you could imagine, a kind of street urchin. Medders may have been over-womaned, but he did have a sexual presence—Nathan couldn't imagine what she saw in Rafe.

Exactly, he could hear Meriwether saying, *You can't!*

"You ain't the Mafia, are you, boy?" Bobo was saying. "You speak English?"

"No sir, boss. I's a-looking for the promised land."

As though on cue Bobo went into his Wayfaring Stranger routine, singling Rafe out of the line-up and presenting him to Nathan in the words of the song "...just a poor wayfaring stranger, a-traveling through this world of woe.... "

And that was true too. There was something waifish about him, the way his hair fell down over his face, his shy smile, the way he held his body, as though he were always prepared to run. You couldn't believe that he was as old as he was. Right in the middle of what was sinister looking about him, Nathan saw something innocent. Perhaps that's what Toni saw too. He liked the young man a lot, even trusted him— up to a point. And the song told the story of what he liked most. Rafe had wandered in a couple of weeks before Farmington opened, having never heard of the place. Charleyboy had picked him up hitchhiking across the Mass Pike with a bed roll. He had done more work to get the place ready than anyone except Nathan himself—which had confirmed his idea that the way Rafe arrived meant that he was supposed to be there. Now, considering the company he was keeping, Nathan wasn't so sure—there were times when he had to believe that if the projection room clique belonged at Farmington, then he didn't.

"I thought this here was the promised land," Rafe said.

"Maybe next year," Nathan said.

"Did you hear that?" Bobo said. "He said it again!"

An unspoken compromise evolved: Nathan agreed to get off their backs if they would get off his. When he was all but sure that that was how it was being handled, he caught Toni McHugh by herself one day and asked for confirmation.

"Let's make a truce?" he said.

She looked as though she couldn't believe his candor. Her lips parted slowly with an unvoiced *wow*, her hands went into her hip pockets. She was smiling.

"You got anything against truces?" he asked her.

"In general," she said.

He laughed. "What?"

"Truces are always the biggest defeat in the war."

He thought about that for a minute. "Not necessarily."

She thought about that for a minute. "Okay. As long as they're made in full appreciation."

"Sounds right to me," he said.

"In full appreciation of the time to come," she said.

"When there won't be any need for them any more."

"No. When they get to be broken. That's what truces are for, isn't it —all that delicious anticipation?"

He laughed again. "I think we just negotiated the terms."

"I think you're right," she said.

"Let's shake on it," he said, offering her his fist.

When she toasted him with her own, his thumb popped up like a cork. His fist was twice as big as hers, more.

"It's a deal," she said.

"It's dealt with," he said.

He was a month into the summer before he realized what it meant to be in charge at Farmington. He was surrounded by people he couldn't talk to.

What all that well-intentioned effort to get through to Makar amounted to was a great cloud of black smoke pouring out of the tail end of the Farmington trip and hanging around the fireplace, like the fallout of any free enterprise: it was their element, they hardly knew they were in it. Into that miasma of white liberal rationality and sympathy and love and sincerity, Jerry one day walked straight, and, where he and Bobo and everybody else turned back before, kept going. For most of a long afternoon Jerry stayed after Makar, no threats or bribes or equivocations, just up front, where they had all been trying to get, this was the real thing: said to Makar's face what everybody was saying behind his back, like how come he didn't take his turn on the kitchen crew, how come he didn't work with the rest of them on Wednesday mornings, cutting grass and painting and weeding the garden and digging the Wish Hole for Rafe's play, how come he didn't come to any of the readings, how come he hadn't read or performed himself, why had he come to Farmington in the first place if he didn't want to know others and to be known. Kept after him for most of a long rainy afternoon, caught him even, by his own robes blowing in his own ostentatious wind—Makar caught, nobody could believe it— even brought him in a ways, loosened him up, loosened *Makar* up, incredible! Word spread quickly—by dinner everybody knew what had happened, and everybody was impressed mightily with Jerry and encouraged about Makar and the future of Farmington. Jerry, a piano student at Harvard, was nearly everyone's idea of the world's dearest young man—gentle, bright, kind, handsome, polite, pleasant absolutely honest and out in the open about everything—a granny would have adored him. But then she would have adored a lot of the people at Farmington, most of them, love and peace, they really meant it. Granny-love did not score with Makar, though, nothing like it, and Jerry did—there was more to him, something tough at the core. He took the next step, and the next, a timid person who overcame his timidity, becoming large and strong in the process, somebody that this crazy black man ended up dealing with. Jerry was probably the only person there who could have gotten away with coming on to Makar like that. He was more simply and thoroughly committed to Farmington than any of them (even Nathan, who had the hesitations of his age, and the preoccupations, finally, of a family man and an artist). Jerry was so perfectly guileless and selfless, call it innocent, that it was impossible to brush him off, even for Makar, so it proved, to be unmoved by his honesty and sincerity, so it seemed. Jerry asked him straight simple questions, and he got some of them answered after a fashion, replete with suggestions that maybe Makar was not so unwilling to play the Farmington game as he had seemed.

Which was born out the very next morning when there appeared on the bulletin board a notice from Makar announcing the first rehearsal of "Pluto," what he called "a sound play," a work of his own art which he was prepared to share with the community. Everybody was pleased and excited, word flew up and down the hill like a dove. At lunch that same day he passed out five scraps of folded paper, a name written in pencil on the outside and a letter on the inside. Warren got P, Suzie got L, Dick got U, Nathan got T, and Rhonda got O. That was all—he didn't explain what he was doing, just rose from his seat while the dessert was being passed out and threaded his way among the six tables to hand out with a smile and a hint of a bow the five scraps of paper with the five names on the outside and the five letters inside. He had never done anything like that before, never even gotten out of his seat at the head of the head table until everyone else had left the dining room and he had sat there alone for upwards of an hour sipping tea and staring out the door. So the very fact that he was up and among them was enough to bring the room to near silence and everyone's attention to bear on what was happening—which no one understood at first, but which everyone figured out in short order. Five people had been cast in "Pluto," that was what was happening, and for further information attend the first rehearsal that afternoon at two in the Music Shed. No one could make much sense out of the cast, the particular five—with the exception of Medders, who was a far-out sound play type, whatever a sound play was—but they were all strangely honored to be selected, and they were all determined to meet Makar more than half way. Even after the rehearsal, where they discovered that their letters were their scripts, that was all there was, there weren't no more, you're P, now get on with it; found out that and very little else. Some rehearsal—nobody was ever going to accuse Makar of over-directing. They figured out among themselves what they were supposed to do, or more exactly what might be done with a P in a sound play, and then wondered later if perhaps Makar weren't far enough out pedagogically to have orchestrated it that way. So Suzie agreed to sing though she couldn't sing, and Nathan agreed to sing though he couldn't sing, and Dick agreed to play his flute though he thought the whole thing was just more Makar jibberish, likely conceived to make fools of them all; they all agreed to go along, congratulating one another on their patience and know-how, on the future of Farmington and of America, and of human relations. When the notice went up for the second rehearsal there had been written on it, and then erased, Please Be Prompt—nobody had been late the first time, what was this—erased, but not so as you couldn't see it, plainly. So everybody in the cast hustled up to the Music Shed at two o'clock prompt—and for an hour or so, while waiting for Makar to show up, they tooted around practicing "Pluto," voice and flute. They played the piano, they held sheet music up to the sun looking for watermarks; they whistled, twirled imaginary key chains, worked up little soft shoe parodies of nonchalance. They hung around for an hour or so analyzing their reactions and their responsibilities—and then, as the afternoon wore thin and Makar never showed, please be prompt indeed, they drifted off feeling by turns foolish and angry.

He did not show until supper time. There he came slowly up out of the woods, dressed in his robes: everybody knew he was coming, the mojo navigator himself, but nobody was looking. When he got to the flagstone terrace outside the dining room, Warren Medders was right there at his side, like a pennant-race manager after a bad call, shaking the rules of fair play in his face. "Where in the hell have you been!" To everyone's consternation, Medders was wearing an African robe of his own, the price tag still wired to the hem in the back like a prehensile tail. Nobody was moving, not a sound, they were not even looking at one another. He had gone cryptic! cryptic! one step better, maybe one step too far. He had gotten the robe that morning in Northampton, and while he was gone someone stole his dope and fifty dollars. He was upset, and in more ways than he approved of or could get straight yet, for in addition to his dope and his money he was missing his wife too now, starting to miss her. That morning she had told him she was moving into the projection room with Rafe. He had gone to Northampton in turmoil. He had bought the robe in a cool fit. He still didn't know what he was doing, but you could never tell it by the way he was acting. The Harvard dialectician had taken over, as it always did in his times of stress, accomplished in reason and the laws of evidence: Warren J. Medders, junior Phi Beta Kappa, summa cum laude, a master's degree in musicology from Yale, his compositions performed widely and reviewed in *The New York Times*, and for the last two years Composer in Residence at Oberlin. He believed that Makar stole his dope and his money (which was not the case—Toni took them by mistake, didn't even know she had them yet), and he believed that Makar was off somewhere adding on insults by smoking his dope and spending his money while he and the rest of the cast were promptly tooting around the Music Shed that afternoon, doing as they indeed had been told. Medders went into him broadside, revving with logic like a buzz saw. Professional jealousy was suspected now by some, but no one had any idea what he was doing in an African robe—except Toni, who out of respect for his pain and confusion had absented herself from dinner; and Nathan, who knew almost immediately what was going on, hadn't for a minute believed there would be no suffering. The feeling was, the robe would not have been right even if Makar *wasn't* there (which Medders himself agreed with, once the worst of it was over). Makar answered all his questions and demands with silence. He wasn't ever going to get along with the resident composer, especially a white one that wore African robes, especially not today. Where he had been he wasn't saying: elsewhere, that much for sure: on the flats, running barefoot perhaps, or in a bar ditch on all fours, cattails and marsh grass, watching his hands under water. Following him step for step, sitting down next to him at the table and staying there throughout the meal, Medders reasoned his anger into Makar's ear as though it were the law, pointed all kinds of fingers, Cupid's whole quill full—while thirty-seven people in the same room shoveled their food and pretended not to listen. Things were cut loose now. For weeks everybody had been tiptoeing around the head table, then cryptic! cryptic! and now Medders in African robes of his own, the first public cuckold of the summer, declaring yet another war on arrogance and ignorance. It was a drama. Every now and then Makar raised his hand and said "Peace, peace." And he meant it too, he wanted this angry white man to shut his fast mouth and let them all eat in peace.

"Peace," Makar said, "peace."

But Medders stayed right after him.

The next day at lunch Makar tapped his water glass with a knife while the dessert was being put to the table and rose from his seat, the old catch-me-if-that's-what-you-think-you're-doing smile on his face. They had come a long way, the Farmington Community of the Arts, they were going to be a successful experiment yet: Makar himself tapping the water glass and addressing the group! Everybody fell immediately silent. Makar said that no one should feel obliged to be in "Pluto," that anybody who wanted out should feel free. "You know what I mean?" he said. And he smiled. And they did. He meant that all the people who thought that he was full of shit should cut their losses and split forthwith, which was a lot of them now. He went on to say what most of them already knew because it was a big deal in Farmington's public relations: that "Pluto" was going to be performed as part of the Annual Music Festival at the Chesterfield Community Church in less than a week: there was time enough for only one or two more rehearsals. But still no one should feel obliged, everyone should feel free—no hard feelings. "You know what I mean?" he asked them. No one could back out now without undercutting Nathan and the whole community. They had asked to hear his music, and they were going to hear it now whether they wanted to or not—in fact, they were going to make his music for him, as best they could. He was smiling, looking around the room, smiling. It was like one of those lop-sided tilted mirror-rooms at the funhouse on Mt. Tom: you didn't know which way to lean, vertigo. People were beginning to feel more than they understood: they knew what he meant if they wanted to, maybe even if they didn't. He had them now, and they were becoming aware of it.

Both Chesterfield policemen were out in the intersection under the flashing yellow light directing the annual music festival traffic. One of them was a small old man whose hat and gun were too big, the most officious man in town—when Nathan was a kid in Memphis, they used to call him Willie the Weasel. In their Sunday clothes families were converging on the church from all directions, exchanging pleasantries—young children with freshly polished shoes, highschool couples holding hands, a young crew-cut marine on furlough, an old lady in a wicker wheelchair pushed by her white-haired daughter, middle-aged couples with their Bibles, farmers, shop keepers, the town fathers, some of them so far out of style they were almost back in again. They had invited the Farmington Community because it was the neighborly thing to do, and also because they wanted to expose themselves to the finer things in life. There was about it all something of two tribes coming together, acting out the ritual of having heard of each other.

On the wall of the vestibule just inside the door, lighted by spotlights made of coffee cans, was a big map of the world, surrounded by snapshots of all the Chesterfield boys in uniform; each picture was connected by braided red, white and blue plastic to a gold star on the map which marked the spot where the boy (Pfc. William "Billy" Lowell, First Cavalry, DaNang, South Vietnam) was now serving; and above the map a big red, white and blue sign saying, Write Our Boys Overseas.

"What's happening, daddio?" Bobo asked Makar, trying to usher him along with the crowd on into the church proper. "Getting any gravel for your goose?"

"Mum's the word," Makar said, refusing to look at anybody. Carrying his red velvet robe on a hanger, wearing his red velvet hat, he waited for the passageway to clear before he entered.

Through the second door they were greeted by an impeccably neat Negro woman in her middle years: her hair was straightened, she was wearing a plain dress that came down below her knees and comfortable shoes with half heels and, a touch of stylishness, blue plastic glasses with sequins. Smiling, she handed them a mimeographed piece of blue paper which read, "Folk Music is a song of the folk, their dreams and aspirations. The thought that the Negro might have released or fixed to adopt Christianity, and that there were several good reasons for such an outcome, one being the vast gulf between the Christianity practiced by those who preached it, leads to curious speculations there would have been no Negro spirituals. A. Crucifixion—B. Love—C. Shout— "

In their seats the Farmington contingent, full of excitement—dread of what was likely to happen mixed with exhilaration over what could —read it more carefully, conceding finally that that was indeed what it said.

The first act was a barbershop quartet that had been worked up hurriedly to fill in for a soloist who had gotten sick. In white shirts and black leather bow ties and dark blue pants and white socks they stood elbow to elbow; two had crew cuts, but the third had sideburns down to the ear lobes. Out of song books held uniformly high they sang "a song by the famous English poet, Robert Burns." The next act was a handsome young shapely Negro woman in a white sequined gown who, accompanied by her mother on the piano (bringing to mind the possibility that the entire Negro population of Chesterfield was there, not to be out-done by Farmington), recited a poem about the creation of the world in a rich theatrical voice; at the end she bowed, her straightened hair falling in front of her like a curtain. The third act was the Chesterfield pharmacist of forty years; he played the violin from a score on a high school music stand, accompanied by his next-door neighbor and accompanist of twenty-eight years, Mrs. James Cramer, her husband Jimmy—also introduced—smiling from the third pew aisle. Next were the spirituals, the hand-out lady accompanied by the other two Negroes. And next was a sound play called "Pluto" by Makar Atnui Aknada of the Farmington Community of the Arts.

Makar came out first, alone, walking more quickly than usual, the brown corduroy drawstring bag hanging at the end of his arm like an outsized boxing glove. He acted as though he had something particular on his mind: scooted right out onto the stage and circled the pulpit, slowing down suddenly, attentive now, testing its powers: and then, in ever-expanding circles, tested the candelabra, the flower stands, the organ, the high-backed preacher's chair: making his obscure orbits and laying his obscure claims on the place. No one in the church except perhaps Sinclair, Medders and Toni McHugh—who were off stage waiting with the rest of the cast for the cue to enter—had the slightest idea what he was doing. Makar was wearing his long red robes, and his pointed red elf hat, but he was not acting like it. He was strangely businesslike, more the waiter than the head of the head table. He undid the mysterious brown corduroy bag perfunctorily and took out a curved hunting horn and blew it—just like that, no ceremony. Blew it once, and then slam-bang stuffed it back in the bag. And just stood there, staring off into the distance. For a moment it appeared that he was going to slow things down, to become deliberate, to start acting as though he was part of a performance—but he did not. He fished a harmonica out of the bag, and ran it cursorily across his mouth, and then fished out of the bag one after another a whole entourage of noise makers, jangled and whistled and pumped and tooted and rattled each one of them once in the most perfunctory

manner, stuffing it immediately back into the bag and pulling out
another until just as suddenly as he began he was done, discarding the
bag on the floor next to the highback chair. He then went over to the
organ, gathered his robes so he could sit, and sat, with his back to the
audience. The Farmington people out there were getting antsy. Not
even Nathan, who had been to a Chesterfield Annual Music Festival
(back when Farmington was a school instead of a community and he
was a teacher instead of a resource), was prepared for how out of place
they all were. He should have asked Jerry to play Beethoven, or even
Schoenberg, or Morty to sing arias, or Sinclair to play Ives—anything
but this. In Chesterfield, Pluto was not even the farthest out planet, but
Mickey Mouse's good old lovable dog, and Makar was not giving
them any help at all. In fact he was confusing his own cast. When he sat
down at the organ and arranged his robes it appeared for a moment
yet again as though something were about to begin, but he was just as
perfunctory at the organ as he had been with the noise makers. He
played a few notes, and then a few chords, and then he merely sat
there. For a full minute or so, without moving, his back to the audience, he just sat there. Then he played again, this time with the backs
of his hands, and his elbows, but there seemed to be no intent to that
either: it was not irreverent or funny or histrionic: it was nothing, just
more messing around with everybody waiting. And then he left the
organ and went to the highback chair off to the side of the pulpit and
took his seat.

And the minute he sat down in that chair everybody knew that the
performance had begun.

It was several minutes yet before he gave the signal for the cast to file
in, but the moment Makar took that chair, shutting his eyes as he
lowered himself slowly down, something changed: he gave the whole
church a spin, erasing all the static: suddenly everything was absolutely
still and charged with expectation. You saw now, for the first time,
that he was barefoot. His ankles were crossed: his arms laid like those
of a statue on the arms of the chair: his chin up: his head laid back: his
black face glazed with sweat: his bulging eyes shut. And he sat there,
exactly like that, without even breathing it seemed, for a long time, as
though he and the chair were carved together, everyone in the church
staring at him: locked: just him and each of them: as somehow they
had always feared it would be.

Then a noise came out of him, half moan, half shout. His lips did not move, but this unearthly noise came out of him, and startled everyone. They were all looking around to see where it had come from—as the cast filed in from the side and "Pluto" began.

For a while the Chesterfield congregation was polite, watching attentively, familiar enough with the foreignness of the finer things of life. But soon they got restless. Toni McHugh, filling in for Rhonda who was sick, was performing at Makar's feet, addressing him with a body of O's. That was too much. They knew what that meant if they wanted to know, perhaps even if they did not. There in their church a woman in tights was dancing for a black man, right there where the pulpit ordinarily stood.

Toni was the key to what was happening for the Farmington people as well. With her reputation for no nonsense none of them would have been surprised in the least had she refused even to attend "Pluto," and there she was, the only true volunteer in the cast, squirming around on the floor at Makar's feet, very much the dancing girl in someone else's script. The mere fact of her participation was enough to make some take it more seriously than they would have otherwise—the spirit in which she performed was making it impossible for anyone from Farmington to dissociate himself.

The whole cast was into it now. What began as a kind of late 60's sport—with the freaks as cheerleaders, give em a P give em an L give em a U U U, with the homecoming king on his throne, the head skirt doing O after O at his naked feet—was now breathing more deeply, running with its eyes shut toward another kind of home altogether: this play, these people, this church, this afternoon. Nathan was wandering up the aisle with a flashlight, a glazed look on his face: up the stem of P after P Nathan of all people came, ferris-wheeling into the circles, his head thrown back and his eyes closed and his mouth wide with P's. That big bearded administrator was having fun for a change, fun! Cut the checklists, Nathan, cut the schedules and the master plans and let her rip! On he came, into the universal plosive, broadcasting concentric circles of perfectly spaced-out sound—a little big bang of creation, lightning flashing from his hand. While the rest of the cast did likewise, sounding out the other parts in the other aisles, King Spacey himself, down there where the received word was spoken, eyes closed and shining face thrown back in an audience, seemed to bring it all together with his silence.

A grey-haired woman in front of Meriwether turned to her husband

and said that she thought they were a bunch of dope fiends. All over the church now the congregation was whispering, protesting Makar and his art.

And out of that mix Farmington for the first time came together, a community of sorts. They were scattered all over the back half of the church, in threes and fours: Meriwether glanced at Ellie and David, and the three of them glanced at Bobo and Rafe, and all five of them glanced at Lolly who was looking at them, and everybody looked at Nathan, for christsakes look at Nathan would you! Look at Medders! The white church on the green was not saying anything that they themselves had not said, hardly, but they weren't about to sit there and let a bunch of philistines badmouth their Makar and his art!

Here came Medders up the aisle in slow pursuit of T: somnambulistically, his arms stretched out in search of adoption, up the nave of that fine letter he went, his deep voice spiriting out symmetrically along the transept, aspiration after aspiration, his dialectics gone into a play of sound. *Taker?* he could have been saying. *Today?* He too had a flashlight, held out at arm's length like a curious wand: on row after row of evasive faces he shone his light, searching the vast gulf within them. He was the auctioneer of dreams, looking for a bid. Leading to curious speculation indeed, the thought that the Negro may have released or fixed....

Here we are, Medders, here we are—you're home, baby, shine that light over here! The whole Farmington group was together now, conjoined with Makar and by Makar—or so they thought—dancing in high mid-air over the heads of Chesterfield, the song of parts, oh oh ohhh that music of the eliptical spheres! For every hope today there was a possibility, letter by letter, for every heart today there was a whole word! We're here, their spirits sang, we're here! The revolution is working! Don't worry, Granny, we believe in God again!

Afterwards, those who were offended went home, and the rest gathered in the basement and ate fried chicken left over from the benefit supper the night before. They mixed, the neighboring communities, shared whatever could be shared for a while. It was neat. Nathan and Meriwether and Rafe and Toni and Medders and Bobo and Suzie and the rest were waiting to congratulate Makar. They stood around congratulating themselves, stroking what happened, but Makar didn't show, and didn't show, and still didn't show. They went looking for him finally, but he was nowhere to be found. It occurred to several of them that perhaps he was not so pleased or impressed with "Pluto" as they were, but no one wanted to believe that, no one wanted even to say it.

He was swimming in a creek some distance away. When the performance was over he had ducked out the back way and across the lawn, the grass cool and sexy to his bare feet, slipped around the side of the tall white church and proceeded quickly across the front lawn. Then he saw Willie the Weasel directing traffic there in the intersection. It was as though he ran flat into a wall. He was moving out, leaving the church and the performance and picking up momentum as he went, and then he saw the little old man with the big gun. He did not break stride, you would never have known from watching him that anything had happened: his body continued without a hitch, head high and robes flowing, the corduroy bag in one hand and his sandals in the other: but Makar himself stopped dead in his tracks like a creature: alert, perfectly alert, his peripheral vision working suddenly like a good breast stroke. For the next couple of minutes, as he walked across the lawn of the church and past the gun and down the road, he was wired up and ready, in register, not a thought in his head, his moves on base brain. That the man was a cop meant nothing—that he was armed, everything. As Makar passed through the intersection, bare feet on warm gravel, the policeman said, "How are you doing?" and Makar, his head and shoulders thrown back, his robes lifting out behind him like curtains in a breeze, said, "Pretty fair for a square." They smiled at one another, Willie the Weasel and Uncle Tom-Tom, mum's the word. And Makar passed on down the road and out of sight.

That was all that happened at the Chesterfield intersection at the end of that barnswallow evening, as far as met the eye.

Makar was running now, picking up speed as he went. He left the road, leaped the ditch, and ran for a quarter of a mile or so parallel to the stone fence, then suddenly jumped it and continued on into the woods, picking up the pace a little. Although he was barefoot and wearing those long robes and the woods were dense with brush and fallen trees, he ran smoothly, managing to keep from getting snagged or tripped up or even thrown off pace but occasionally, using the corduroy bag as a kind of shield, its weight as a balance. He ran without stopping for twenty minutes, a good part of the way through the woods, and came finally, as the light began to fail, to a stream. He unclothed and lay his robes out neatly on the grass and stood up straight, his naked body a black sheen of sweat. He was wearing a shoulder holster, a gun strapped under his arm next to his heart. The leather was soaked with sweat. He unbuckled it, and without opening his eyes let it drop, catching it on the instep of his left foot and tossing it gently to the ground next to his robes. Then he opened his eyes, checked the scene on all sides, and slipped into the cool water with a loud sigh of pleasure—and stood there on the bank watching himself turn slowly, sensuously, in the clear running water.

Later that night he appeared at the Captain's Den, a roadhouse on the way into Northampton, and hid in the parking lot bushes until Toni and Rafe and Bobo left, and then went in and took a stool at the bar. He was wearing a pea jacket and a blue cloth cap with a bill. He came there several times a week to drink beer and play pool, always alone, hiding outside whenever anybody from Farmington was there. Without a word the bartender brought him a pitcher of beer and returned to the television at the other end of the bar.

Makar was sitting there with his eyes shut a few minutes later when three young white men came in and took stools on either side of him, the third standing behind him, off a half step to the side. All three were athletic and self-assured, smiling, white teeth, trim, attractive, casual on the surface, but only on the surface. There was nothing casual about what they were up to. Makar had never seen them before, any of them, but he knew immediately what was happening.

They were dressed like college boys, faded jeans, sneakers without socks, heavy sweaters, but they were too old to be college boys. One wore an Indian head band, but on him it bore no trace of freakiness.

"Hello, Joe!" the one to his left said.

"Hello, Joe!" the one to his right said.

"Hello, Joe!" the one behind him said.

Makar shut his eyes, becoming absolutely motionless.

"Where you living now?" the leader said.

And the other two chimed in, "Where you living now?" one right after the other, "Where you living now?"

He was like a pinball, caught in a tight triangle of bumpers.

He did not respond.

There was a silence.

They were waiting.

The two who were seated had their elbows on the bar and were leaning forward, heads propped on their hands, faces turned so that they were looking straight at him, mirror images of one another, and the third was leaning forward, his foot on the back of Makar's stool, staring at the floor with a smile. Periodically he leaned in and made himself felt against Makar's ribs.

They waited.

"Come on, Joe, that ain't no way to act."

"Come on, Joe, that ain't no way to act."

"Come on, Joe, that ain't no way to act."

The leader had a deep southern accent, which the other two picked up slightly. Talking very quietly, so that no one else in the bar could hear, they ran where-you-living-now through again, twice, with only a brief pause, and then they fell silent again, smiling, waiting. For several minutes they sat there like that without saying anything, the black man in the middle, motionless. Makar never opened his eyes. South Mouth got three mugs and they poured themselves beer from Makar's pitcher, sliding it back and forth in front of him on the bar. There were five other people in the Captain's Den, all of them at the far end watching a color TV which was on a shelf above the mirror. The eleven o'clock news was on, first Vietnam, then Washington, then the anti-war movement in Boston, Miami and San Francisco. The men watched the news and finished Makar's beer.

When the news was over, they asked whether he wanted to play pool, and he opened his eyes and got off the stool slowly without looking at them and went to the table in the other room and found his cue and stood facing the wall as he chalked the tip.

South Mouth came in carrying a pitcher of beer and four mugs, a lovely smile on his face, and they racked the balls and lagged for break.

Toward the end of the first game, which South Mouth was winning, two of them boxed Makar in again while the third was taking his turn and came at him from both sides.

"Shit, Joe, you wouldn't be putting us on, would you?"

"Shit, Joe, you wouldn't be putting us on, would you?"

He had not looked at any of them yet, or said a word, and still he did not, nothing.

"Shit, Joe, we heard you was first nigger stick. How come you so unfriendly?"

"Yeah, Joe, we heard you was first nigger stick. We come all this way to see you play pool and here you are hacking around letting a bunch of white boys beat you. How come you so unfriendly?"

South Mouth came over, working his smile like he was on TV, and said, "Nigger Joe done turned white and died. Is that where you're living, Nigger Joe, turned white and died?" Makar was watching him now, their eyes were locked on each other. "I think Nigger Joe wants to make the game interestin'. I think he's the kind of nigger that won't play first stick unless the game's interestin'."

He reached into his sweater.

But before he could get his hand out Makar had him pinned to the wall with his cue.

The other two moved in and broke them up immediately.

"Now wait a minute, motherfucker," South Mouth said, "don't get excited. I was just going to make the game interestin'." He got a fold of bills out of his breast pocket and turned the pages, five twenties. But Makar shook him off. He turned five more, and Makar shook him off again, and he turned five more. Makar was sweating.

"I ain't got no money," he said.

"Where you living now, motherfucker?" South Mouth said.

"Where you living now, motherfucker?"

"We'll take an I-owe-you," South Mouth said.

"How's that?" Makar said.

"We'll take an I-owe-you."

They were staring at one another, Makar and South Mouth.

"Un-huh. Un-huh." He chuckled and smiled. "You'll take I.O.U. is what you're saying? I.O.U. three hundred? My pappy, he told me I oughn't never play with strangers, you know what I mean?"

"We just want to see you play, that's all."

"You talking about me writing my name down on a piece of paper. You talking about me writing my name down on I.O.U. three hundred. I don't never write my name down, you know what I mean?"

"Forget about the I-owe-you," South Mouth said. "We just want to see you play, that's all."

South Mouth was smiling again. Waiting and smiling. "Word of honor," he said.

"That's very interestin', what you saying there. You saying you want to bet me three hundred dollars on a pool game, is that right? That's all you saying? You want to bet the only nigger in twenty miles all that money on a pool game? What happens if I win? What happens out in the parking lot? A man take that kind of money he might end up beholden."

"You don't have to worry about anything," South Mouth said.

"That kind of money, somebody always end up sucking cock, you know what I mean? End up somebody thinking somebody else is beholden. White boys come around with a big pocket full of daddy's money, they might want a nigger to suck cock. You know what I mean?"

"We just want to see you play," South Mouth said. "That's all there is to it. You've got my word."

"You got the word, huh, and you giving it to me? Un-huh. Un-huh. The word's money, and you're giving it to me, is that what you're saying? Maybe daddy's money wants to suck nigger cock. Maybe that's what happens in the parking lot? Is that what you come all this way for?"

The three exchanged glances. South Mouth was smiling again, he was beaming. "Nigger Joe ain't turned white and died, no sir!" he said, shaking his head in appreciation. "Ain't dead at all!"

"Four hundred," Makar said.

"You're on!" South Mouth said. And then, hesitatingly, as though he was not sure he ought to be saying it, "Every man's got his price."

"That's right," Makar said. "You just never know what it is until you get to know the man, you know what I mean?"

While the balls were being racked, Makar leaned his cue next to the side pocket and went to the men's room and locked the door and climbed up on the sink and then the toilet stall and out a little window high on the wall. He dropped to the ground and slipped quickly into the bushes and circled the parking lot. He was hiding in the woods where he could see them when they came rushing out the door. They knotted up for a moment in confusion, then fanned out running in different directions.

Makar followed South Mouth, who checked the cars in the parking lot, and then took off down a path that ran parallel to the highway; trailed twenty or thirty yards behind, off to the side, in the bush. The path led to a road-side rest area that was deserted. South Mouth checked the women's room, he did not even bother with the men's, then plunged off into the bush on the other side of the clearing. Makar did not follow; he went into the men's room, urinated, washed his hands, combed his hair, wiped the sweat off his face with a paper towel, straightened and brushed his clothes in the mirror. When he was done he remained facing the mirror and tilted his head back and shut his eyes and breathed deeply, slowing himself down, one slow deep breath through his nose and then another. His stomach swelled with the inhalation, slowly, and then his nostrils flared, his whole body backing down. The circuits were opening, the call was going through, gathering him home as it went.

When South Mouth came into the men's room, breathing hard, he stopped short and froze. Makar was still in front of the mirror, his head tilted back, his eyes shut. Neither of them moved.

The bugs were popping against the overhead light.

A trailer truck went by on the highway, shifting down into a lower gear.

When Makar spoke, still facing the mirror, his eyes still closed, it was with a sardonic white voice.

"Well, well, well, what have we here! I do wish you would look! How are you, Johnny, where have you been, you blackguard, I thought of this meeting daily, rehearsed my lines, thought every time that I turned around that you would be there. My god, how are you, come in, come in, you musn't mind me, I do the best I can, and God knows that it isn't good enough. You realize of course that I have at you daily in my thoughts, murder you, if thoughts isn't too dignified a word for what passes through my poisonous brain. You will have to excuse me. I have no manners, have never had, as you know, I'm sure, better than any man alive. But there is one thing we must get clear. There are probably twenty such things, at least, I'm sure there are, and I'm sure that I will never in this life get twenty things clear, but we must try. Don't ask my why. But you are an honorable man, Johnny, and you always fill me with honorable sentiments, always have, always will, I'm sure. And of course lots else besides, Johnny—which I'm sure you know. You are no child, even if you once were, weren't we all. But there *is* one thing. Let's get it out of the way, quickly. In matters of moment between men of honor there is no other way, I'm sure that you will agree. You looked for me in the wrong place. Do you understand what I am talking about? You looked for me a while ago in the wrong place. I will never, ever forgive you for that, never. Do you understand? I realize that you have every reason in the world to expect to find me there, and I am sure that you will someday, but life is very long, very long indeed, it is one thing that few people ever understand, and honor among old friends is the only thing—what does one say?— that makes it tolerable. I trust that I am making myself clear." Makar turned and opened his eyes and faced South Mouth with a smile. "How are you, Johnny?"

The man's name was Johnny. He had never seen Makar before that night, nor Makar him.

The man retreated several steps, putting his back to the wall, and drew his gun.

"We have been in some bad movies, I would be the last to deny it," Makar said, "but I do wish you would put that silly gun up."

He started walking across the room.

"Stay over there!" Johnny said.

"I will *not*!" Makar said. "How is that to talk to an old friend?"

He walked right up to the young man, who put the barrel of the gun against his chest at arm's length.

"Surely you don't expect me to believe that you are going to use that. You shouldn't have even brought it with you. It's *not* what daddy had in mind—you know that."

They were staring at one another, their faces not three feet apart.

"You have every reason in the world to want to kill me, I'm sure of it. And I'm sure that we both would be better off if you did. But you know as well as I do that you are much too decent a man to do that. And that I am much too clever to allow it to happen. Vile is more like it, much too vile. I tried once, Johnny, I used to put the barrel in my mouth each morning instead of shaving, but I only embarrassed myself. When I was young I believed in these melodramas, but then when we are young we believe in many things, more than one can count."

The man's eyes were coming loose.

"Now put up that intolerable gun so we can talk."

Nothing happened and still nothing, the man merely stared at him, his head wobbling ever so lightly—and then he started to put the gun away.

Until that moment everything that Makar had done and said had been in slow motion, as though his voice and body were drugged, calm, deliberate, as though he were happening under water—but then he exploded. He broke the man's wrist, sending the pistol across the room, and flattened him on the concrete floor, knocking him unconscious. When he came to, Makar was standing over him with his own gun drawn. He knelt down, jabbing his knee into the young man's throat, pointing the pistol straight down between his eyes.

"Un-huh," he said. "Un-huh."

He drew a bead and pushed the barrel straight down it, slowly—stopping an inch away, between Johnny's eyes.

"Where *you* living now?" Makar asked him.

He eased up on his knee so the other could breathe.

"Un-huh. Where *you* living now?"

The young man was grimacing and holding his wrist.

"The next time I see you or anybody who looks like you is going to be the last time, you know what I mean? Don't come around me no more. You take that money back and give it to your daddy and tell him that Joe is dead. You got that? Tell him don't send nobody looking for Joe cause Joe is dead. Turned Black and died. You got that? Turned *Black* and died!"

Makar's breathing was easier now, he was slowing down again. A smile came to his face, and the space around him began to expand, and his nostrils began to flare. He unzipped his pants and took out his cock. "Un-huh. You was looking for this wasn't you? Looking for it in the wrong place?" He held it down to the man's south mouth and told him to kiss it. Which he did. He shut his eyes and kissed Makar's cock. "Oh no," Makar said, "you got to see what you're doing in this business. You know that." So the man kissed it again, this time with his eyes open.

"Un-huh," Makar said. "I told you what was going to happen in the parking lot, didn't I? I told you a lot of things—how come you can't listen? How come white folks can't hear nothing but themselves? That's what I want to know."

For several days after "Pluto," nobody saw Makar, nobody knew where he was. And when he did show up again, at a dance being held on the volleyball court, he threatened to destroy what they wanted to believe he had created.

The dance was Bobo's idea, a 1950's sock hop, and he was the m.c., brilliantly. The spirit that had been touched loose in Chesterfield was still with them; they wanted to feel good about one another and the community and to have fun. And they did. Like all good parodists there was within Bobo a simpler version of what he was doing, a real heartfelt high school master of ceremonies, and because Bobo loved him everybody loved Bobo that night and applauded his antics. At ten o'clock the King and Queen of the hop were chosen, names drawn from a hat, and it was Jerry and Rhonda. That put them all to new faith in the stars, for Jerry and Rhonda were not only a couple—figure the odds out of a hat on that one—but the romance of the summer. Right in the middle of the coronation Bobo spotted Makar, who had just returned to Farmington and was watching the dance from his room in the Barn: seated sideways in the window, he was looking down on them over his shoulder, more like a painting than a person, a dark figure framed, immobile, the spirit of the dead. And Bobo, who was using a flashlight as part of his act, shined it directly on him and rubbed it in—as if to say come on, Makar, everybody sees you now, everybody loves you, don't be that way.

Seconds later Makar was there at the sock hop: came marching out of the Barn carrying a broom tucked under his arm, a broom: down the slope and straight up to the crepe streamers that roped off the dance area. One after another people became aware of him there and stopped dancing, stopped talking. His angry voice rose above the music, calling Bobo all manner of bad things. Everyone fell silent. The record played on for a few seconds, then skated down into the rhythmic concentric static at the core. You goddamn hippie, Makar was saying, you honkie punk, shine that motherfucking light on me ever again—And what? There were people there who did not hear because they did not want to hear. But it came around again, and again —each time meant most of all for them. Put that on him again, anything on him ever again, and there would be violence.

People hung around for a while, there was even a brief half-hearted effort to recapture the fun and games, but the sock hop was broken, and so were the hopes born of "Pluto" in the Chesterfield Church. They were eyeball to eyeball now in the school house door, arguing about what to do next, arguing about everything. Right from the start a lot of them had said that they thought he was dangerous, Phyllis Brodsky among them, a psychiatrist with a weighty voice in such matters; and now, with his threat, that seemed less suspect than it once had. Soon it was to be not suspect at all.

Two days after the sock hop, Jerry, who was taking Makar's place on cleanup, was sweeping out the dining room after lunch. Makar had not asked him to take his place, had refused in fact ever to acknowledge that such a place existed, but Jerry always did what had to be done—and more. The floor did not need mopping, but he was putting the chairs up on the tables, preparing to wet mop. The dishes were finished, the garbage tended to, the kitchen cleaned up, everybody had cut out for the afternoon except for a couple of young people who were taking a nap on the couch over by the fireplace—everybody except Makar, who was still at his place, staring out the door into the sunlight.

He had not moved for the last three quarters of an hour except to sip tea from a cup that sat on the table before him. The stained plastic cup formed a perfect triangle with his elbows on the table, the base of a pyramid described by his forearms, his hands joined palm to palm at the tip. He had a thing going with that figure, a feel in his muscles for the engineering of it. Ever so subtly he played the margins, all the transactions of gravity, this way and that, water and air, lean and tilt. He floated into the center, where suspended he positioned himself elsewhere at the same time, flesh shifting down, turning into light: then ascended, in a mirror image of rain, a slow upsway of particles on their way into space: water and the cold swirl of stars, awesome the elegance of that darkness.

When Jerry finished with the rest of the room he asked Makar please to move so that he could sweep under his chair and the table. Makar said that he hadn't finished lunch, to please let him be. Rhonda was there, standing a few feet away with her hands in the hip pockets of her jeans—they exchanged glances, she and Jerry. And then Jerry explained to Makar what he was doing, asked the black man please to move, or at least to lift his feet so that he could do his work. Makar told him please to get away from him with that broom. Again Jerry exchanged glances with Rhonda. Waited for a minute, making sure that neither he nor the black man did anything they did not mean to do. Then he started sweeping under the chair with Makar still in it.

After the music festival, while Makar was swimming in the creek, his gun lying several yards away on the robes in the late afternoon light, the moon rising like a memory of itself in the east, Nathan got a call from California: his friend and mentor, Ortega Bruno, was seriously ill, they feared cancer, at the age of forty-six.

He went straightway into the darkroom, knowing that there, at his work, which owed so much to Bruno, he could best deal with the news. But he suffered one interruption after another. First Melissa, the tap on the door so tentative that he guessed immediately who it was. What she wanted was for him to develop a roll of color film for her, snapshots. She was the most unlikely person there, a child of the forties, and terribly dear to him for that, a weaver and writer of children's stories, timid, unassuming, virginal, a kid sister. Her wealthy parents had driven her all the way from San Diego in a late model Ford station-wagon because they were afraid of airplanes. And, it seemed obvious to Nathan, because they wanted to check out Farmington, and him. He was touched by the bravery of Melissa's wanting to be there, and by the bravery of her parents, who must have thought, despite all he did to reassure them, that they were turning her over to their nightmare. He was careful to keep her from seeing just how outlandish her request was. And then, just as he was getting his concentration back, yet another knock on the door, this one full of urgency. The cook, he was informed, was on the rampage: she had found cat shit in the pantry and was threatening to quit. And he was no more than back from dealing with that when Bobo showed up, excited about a set of new work prints.

What for a moment seemed to be yet another interruption turned into something quite different. He saw himself in Bobo, he saw Bruno in himself—as they spread the prints out on the counter, as they moved them silently about. Bobo was a better photographer than he'd been at that age, and he was not as good a teacher as Bruno had been at his, but the same thing was happening, no interruption at all.

Most of the pictures were of the young people, but there were some of David and Ellie with their children, of Meriwether, of Nathan himself. Again and again the images told him—as Bobo's work always did—that the young man was a lot more mature and perceptive and complex and responsive to others than he acted. All of them had a spontaneity that his own photographs lacked, that he admired and envied. There were three pictures of Meriwether there that were better, no question, than anything he himself had ever done of her—three of them.

That night in bed he told Meriwether, by way of approaching the news of Ortega, about all the interruptions. He didn't want to be hard on Melissa, he was sure that she had no idea what she was asking him to do, but how come, he wanted to know, he was always getting into situations like that?

"You can't act like the corner drugstore and then be put off when people treat you like it," Meriwether said.

He laughed. And pulled her to him.

She resisted him less than he was expecting.

Suddenly he was talking about Bobo, the new pictures, especially the ones of her. One in particular: Bobo had caught her with her chin raised, the middle of a turn. Nathan had forgotten all about Bruno. "I've got a confession to make. I was jealous."

He thought that she would find his confession endearing, as she always had, that sort of thing, but she did not, not at all. When he tried to justify himself, she cornered him, every way he turned. And when he gave up, offering to stand judged, she was no less irritated.

"That's just talk," she said. "You're asking me to treat you like a child. I don't want anything to *do* with your jealousy—I've had too much to do with it already."

"What do you want me to do?"

"I want you to quit asking me what I want you to do. It's not enough to *say* it's weak and crazy, you've got to *feel* it."

"I *do* feel it," he said.

"No, you don't. All you feel is *threatened*. You start out being threatened by Bobo or whoever in the hell, and when that won't work any more you feel threatened by my reaction to you."

"I'm doing the best I can," he said.

"So am I," she said. "For a change."

She took her book and went down to the sunporch to read.

And he got his transistor—stopping in the doorway to tell her about Ortega—and then slipped outside into the dark to listen to the news. He feared that he had used his friend's illness as a play for sympathy, and he feared that she had known it. When the news came on, though, he pressed the radio hard to his ear, oblivious to everything except what was happening in Vietnam.

Later, returning to bed, Meriwether apologized. She was just upset, she told him, her usual bitchy self. He wasn't her problem, nor was Farmington—she was. She said everything about herself that he could say, and more, and said it much more harshly. That always had the same effect on him: he wanted to defend her; which she allowed him to do only up to a point. He was convinced, as he always was at such times, that she would never again be such easy prey to her moods.

It was the closest they had been in weeks, since well before coming to Farmington. He wanted to answer her honesty with a confession of his own. She had no idea that he had been involved in Bobo's arrest—an effort (in part successful) to protect one of Bobo's girlfriends, another of his students, an innocent girl from east Tennessee who was already a speed freak, on the verge of heroin and of dealing. Nor did she have any idea that he had assumed custody so that Bobo could be there. He wanted her to know the whole story—yes, he'd been attracted to the girl; no, he hadn't been to bed with her—but he was afraid of her reaction to it. Instead he told her about a little run-in he had had earlier that week with Bobo and Rafe. They had suggested solving Farmington's financial problems by growing marijuana.

"Oh come *on!*" she said. She was sitting cross-legged in the middle of the bed, her short night gown in her lap.

She was closer to Bobo's age than to his. It was always a relief to him to hear her talk that way about young men.

"You mean Bobo doesn't turn you on?"

Nathan said that with a laugh, putting his hand on her hip.

He knew, the minute he touched her, that she could act as though he had blown it again.

"I just can't help it, Nathan. You know how I am about hippies."

He put his hand on the inside of her knee.

She tugged playfully at his beard. Much as she would like to, she said, she couldn't. She had an infection.

He was relieved to hear that she wanted to.

But now he had to deal with something new—or perhaps it was the same old thing, gone for a minute to change shapes.

"What kind of infection?" he said, trying to sound matter-of-fact.

A swollen gland, it was, a consequence of not bathing regularly. All her problems with Farmington were tied up, she said, with her anxiety about the infection and the frustration of being unable to do anything about it. The doctor had told her to take two long hot baths every day —when the water supply would not permit even two a week.

It was a white lace gown—he could see the thin crotch of her white panties. He wanted to believe that she would not be sitting there like that if there were anything more to it than an infection. Listen, she was saying, do you remember...a smile welling up, first in her mouth, then in her voice. Relieved that he had not depressed her, he welcomed, with only the slightest hitch, the change of subject.

"...at the meeting Friday night, just after we decided on the sign-up sheet for bathing?"

He remembered. Bobo had suggested that they all take showers together, not just to save water but to get to know one another better. He had said, "How's that for getting it all together?" And everyone had laughed.

They laughed again now, remembering.

"Sometimes you really have to admire him," Meriwether said. "He's got only that one damn thing that he does, but he sure knows how to do it. He's got absolutely no shame whatsoever. It wears you down eventually. You end up responding to the sheer unadulterated energy of it. He makes a Baroque work of art out of adolescent dirty-mindedness."

Repeatedly he had tried to get her to give Bobo his due. But now, hearing her talk with feeling about another man, what he heard was her yearning for everything that he was not. No wonder she did not want to make love to him. It was all so depressing—as though this great wad had grown up between them, their marriage reduced now to passing it back and forth.

As he was falling asleep that night, thirty four years old, Ortega's age when they met, his thoughts skating down toward some concentric static at the core, he remembered Makar. Jogging one morning he had come off the ridge, out across the field where the night before they had had a brush-burning party: he was lengthening his stride, beginning to push a little on the way home, to shake himself down and out, to sweat, his attention turning more and more inward. Suddenly Makar was there: poking around in the ashes with a stick. The sky was just beginning to lighten. There was a full moon low in the west, and on the eastern horizon the first broad flush of red. And there they both discovered at the same moment they were: two men alone together out in the middle of an open field: staring at one another—like a film, as Nathan now saw it, stopped on one frame. The stick was poised above the ground like a blind man's cane. Makar's large eyes were fixed on him. At first Nathan was merely startled, but Makar's gaze frightened him—so badly in fact that he did not see what he was looking at. Which he was witnessing now for the first time as the image came back to him on the verge of sleep: Makar was barefoot. He was walking around in the hot ashes barefoot.

Suddenly Nathan was wide awake again: lying on his side in his bed in the still house: staring across the room. For a moment he did not know where he was.

It was not a stick, he saw now, it was a broom, tucked under his arm.

Maybe the ashes were not that hot.

He turned over quickly to hug his wife—but she was not there.

Or in the room.

Mason was asleep in his crib, but Meriwether was gone.

He slipped out of bed and quickly down the stairs. Stood alone on the moonlit floor of his office for a long minute with no idea what he was going to do next. Then slipped quietly through the kitchen and the library and stood where he could see the sunporch without being seen. There she was, sitting in the dark. Sitting in the wicker chair staring out the window and smoking. The tip of the cigarette flared ever so delicately, then smoke around her head in the moonlight. She was alone.

All he could get at that hour was WINS from New York, the twenty-four hour news station. He took his radio into the bathroom and shut the door. In rhythm to his efforts on the toilet he pressed his transistor hard and then harder to the side of his head, as though he were trying to pass the news through his ear into his skull, through his body and out. While he was waiting for the latest report from Southeast Asia it occurred to him that perhaps she did not know that he was lying when he told Rafe and Bobo that he had smoked marijuana, that now she could try it without telling him and believe that she was doing no more than he had already done.

o o o

When Jerry tried to sweep under the chair while Makar was still in it, Makar stood up quickly and slapped him. Jerry was stunned. He was holding the broom with both hands, an afterimage of Makar on the night of the sock hop, incredulous—he could not believe that Makar had slapped him in the face.

So Makar slapped him again, more slowly, hard this time.

And Rhonda screamed.

The two people asleep on the couch were up on their feet. The scene was frozen, and for a moment without sound, details etched in the taut high-pitched suddenness of it all: the expression of disbelief on Jerry's face as his mouth and cheek reddened and the broom fell to the floor: Rhonda's hands to the sides of her head, her eyes wide in fright: Makar calm, his body loose as a dancer's, that look on his face, mocking if you wanted it to be—

Then Rhonda ran to Jerry's side, folded him in her arms, and guided him outside, cursing Makar and promising him that he would be sorry.

Makar picked up the broom, propped it against the table, and sat back down, returning to his triangles.

Soon everybody knew, and the argument was joined in earnest. Since the sock hop those who thought he was dangerous had been closing ranks behind Phyllis Brodsky, and now they were insisting that "something be done." That night after dinner, at which Makar did not show, a lot of people stayed on in the dining room to hash the thing out. Even Meriwether, who had kept out of it until now, said that the situation was intolerable. It came out in the discussion that since the sock hop the three girls living in Van Velder had been afraid to go to sleep because Makar had taken to sitting up all night in the kitchen with a big kettle of steaming water on the stove. As usual nobody knew what he was up to, or how to go about finding out, but Medders pointed out that the Barn where he slept was worse than a barracks, maybe he wanted simply to be where it was warm and comfortable. Then what was the big kettle of water for? Five gallons of boiling hot water for tea? Even if he was up to no harm in the kitchen, there were a lot of people who were afraid of him now, and with good reason, three of them so afraid they couldn't go to sleep at night. It was time for the community to do something about it. The girls had enlisted help from Jerry, who was not only the proven one in dealing with Makar but someone they could trust not to belittle their fears. Charleyboy went down to the kitchen with him, and there Makar was sitting in the cook's chair with his eyes shut rocking back and forth, his hands folded neatly in his lap. They tried to talk to him, but he wouldn't even acknowledge that they were there. If he hadn't been rocking back and forth they would have sworn that he was asleep. So they looked at one another and shrugged, and Jerry started to turn off the gas. At which point Makar without missing a rock said no. He had turned the gas on, and he would turn it off—when he was ready. Jerry went through the whole thing again, explaining how the girls upstairs were afraid to go to sleep; went on in fact, as he had done earlier that summer, told him how his behavior at the sock hop had frightened everybody and was screwing up the whole community. While Jerry was facing everything out for the girls upstairs and for everybody, Charleyboy, out of what he described at the big after-dinner meeting as pure social awkwardness, doodled on the steamed-up windows with his finger. Still rocking back and forth with his eyes shut Makar again called a halt. Evidently he did not see anything social or awkward about it at all: he claimed that Charleyboy was sending messages and told him to get away from that window. "What are you talking about?" Charleyboy said. "I was just doodling!" Makar stopped rocking, but he did not open his eyes. "Un-huh. You ain't going to work that on me. Get your ass away from that window in a hurry!" There Jerry was in the middle of a perfectly reasonable, sincere, straightforward effort to explain to Makar what it meant to live with thirty-nine other people, and they ended up arguing about what Charleyboy was doing writing on the steamed-up windows. And if that wasn't crazy and frustrating enough, something of the same thing happened all over again when Jerry and Charleyboy told the story to everybody there at the big meeting. It fell into the argument at precisely the point where it would seem to carry the day for those who were insisting that something had to be done about Makar, and it ended up turning people against Jerry. It was shut up and quit apologizing all over again. Nobody wanted to attack Jerry or even to accuse him of anything in particular, but several people started wondering out loud about his sweeping under Makar's chair—wasn't there something in his broom and in his midnight policing of the kitchen that implicated him in Makar's hostility? Phyllis Brodsky wanted Makar expelled, and a lot of other people did too now, Meriwether tentatively among them, but all those whose minds weren't made up leaned toward cooling it. "Why don't we all just try leaving him alone for a change?" somebody said. When Nathan, who had seemed impartial until then, seconded that, Phyllis accused him of bad faith. This discussion, she said, was nothing but an escape valve. She wanted the whole thing dealt with again at the regular meeting where a vote could be taken. They all fell then to bickering. It was likely that Makar would have gotten by with slapping Jerry—or more exactly the community would have gotten by it without a major disruption—had that been the end of the violence, but it was not.

A couple of days after the business with Jerry, as it was calming down, Makar laid Bobo out. It was Friday night, late, after a long community meeting about stealing and finances and trust, which had ended in yet another hassle about how the kitchen was run and what they were eating and the possibility of turning the place into a year-round community. Followed by a fireplace rap at Van Velder where Nathan, who was not there, was roundly denounced for doubletalk and for having too much power. Medders summed it up when he said that Nathan wanted everybody to talk as though the place belonged equally to all of them but he didn't want anybody to act as though it did. Farmington was just what some of them were looking for, nearly a hundred acres in the foothills of the Berkshires, nine buildings, several small cabins in the woods. When push came to shove, Medders said, which was going to happen before long if things didn't change, they would find out where everybody really stood. Makar was not there, had not been seen all day, and when the subject turned to him Rhonda started fooling around with Bobo, which sent Jerry into a funk, which got a bunch of people mad at Rhonda and Bobo—who took off their clothes and ran naked holding hands around the dining room, mocking something or other. Everybody got pissed off at them and left; by midnight Van Velder was empty—even the girls who lived upstairs found someplace else to go. Rhonda and Bobo ended up in an empty room in the Barn, reading poetry to one another. They were lying side by side on the bed, naked except for hats, when Makar kicked the flimsy door open.

"What the hell's going on?" Bobo demanded.

"Un-huh," Makar said. "Un-huh."

Bobo got off the bed and demanded again an explanation.

Makar asked him to step outside.

Bobo told him to leave.

Makar told him to take off his glasses.

"Get the hell out of here!" Bobo said. "This is my room."

"Ain't nothing here belongs to you, boy. Take off them glasses or I'm going to bust em all over your hippie face."

"I'm using the goddamn room, now get *out!*"

"How come you ain't got on no shirt?"

Makar stripped off his dashiki and tossed it behind him into the hall.

"Just get out!"

"How come you ain't got on no pants?"

He dropped his pants, stepped out of them, and kicked them away.

"Leave us alone," Rhonda said. "We're not bothering you."

Makar took a step toward Bobo, and Bobo retreated.

"Un-huh. Un-huh. You been running your mouth all summer, how come you ain't running your mouth now? Done run out of SDS, is that what you're saying? I'll run you out of more'n SDS!"

He slapped Bobo in the face, knocking his hat and glasses off. Rhonda screamed. And he slapped him again, knocking him up against the wall.

Makar shut his eyes then, and went into a dance, a crazy loose-jointed finger-snapping gig, a little buck-and-wing, hambone, karate, a lot of Makar, his naked arms and legs waving around like tentacles. He looked as though he were conducting some weird music, more comic than violent, but every time an arm flew out or a leg Bobo was at the other end of it, getting slapped and kicked around the room. You could hardly believe that his eyes were shut, but they certainly appeared to be, tight. In a half-squat with his knees spread wide, his thick lips a blur, he was snapping his fingers and clapping his hands and slapping his naked thighs—only it was in slow motion, trance-like, his loose-jointed arms and legs waving about as though he were under water. Bobo reeled this way and that, ducked, tried to stay out of reach and when he couldn't he flailed back, but every time Makar swung, blind as it seemed, Bobo was there to take another stinging open-handed slap, sweat flying—not particularly hard, the blows, but loud. He was bleeding now, at the mouth and nose, and Rhonda was screaming, but for all the blood it was more a spanking than a beating. Finally Makar stopped, stood up straight, opened his eyes, and told Rhonda, quietly, to shut up.

She was hysterical, screaming first at him then for help.

"Hush up!" he shouted at her.

And she did, immediately.

"Un-huh. Un-huh."

Then he left.

Bobo was sitting in the middle of the floor, his head between his knees.

From up in the graveyard came sounds of a small party, several people laughing and dancing.

Nathan tried to hold off, to let things cool down, but there was no way. An emergency meeting was held the next morning after breakfast in the dining room, and everybody except Makar and Toni was there. Jerry spoke first, told the story of being slapped, which everybody knew, and the story of the rocking chair and the stove, which some did not. And Charleyboy told of doodling on the window and being accused of putting a hex on Makar. And then Bobo told his story, getting punched out for reading poetry. There was a lot of head-shaking, the sheer outrageousness of it, for reading *poetry!* There was no doubt now that something had to be done, it was merely a question of what. Phyllis Brodsky, the three girls who lived there in Van Velder, and several others, including Meriwether, were on record for expulsion. Much of what Phyllis had predicted weeks ago had come to pass, people were being forced to face that, and now she was saying that either they would deal with him or somebody was going to get killed or maimed. Jerry spoke again, saying that things had gone too far, he'd tried everything, he was with Phyllis now. And then Rhonda. And John. One after another people sided with Phyllis, some with vehemence, like Sara, who had been outspoken in her opposition to Phyllis last time; others, like David, with great reluctance. It was a defeat for the community to come to this, he said, but he didn't see any other solution. Bobo did: he wanted to call the cops: he said if the community didn't deal with Makar that was exactly what he was going to do. He was the last person at Farmington you would expect to want cops, and it led several more people to side with expulsion.

Finally someone took exception. Joe Lainard, who had been raised on the streets of a Bridgeport slum, said that he could not get all that excited about somebody getting punched out. He seldom talked in these meetings—his words had special weight, for everyone. And Sinclair seconded him—said that it was no big deal, that they were all supposed to be grownups now, capable of solving their own problems. And Medders joined them: sounded, he said, like a lot of suburban hysteria. They didn't want to call the cops, they wanted to become the cops. He pointed out that Bobo and Rhonda had been running around the place naked, which could be construed as a pretty unfriendly thing to be doing to Makar.

"Then what in the hell are we supposed to do?" someone asked.

"Just cool it," Medders said.

"Horseshit!" Bobo said. "I didn't do anything to him!"

"Just stay *away* from him," Joe Lainard said.

"Live down *here* and talk like that!" Rhonda said.

"You're damn right!" several of the young people said.

"You guys up the hill don't know what it's like to *live* with him. You go to bed at night, and that's that!" Rhonda said. "We have to *live* with him, and by *your* goddamn rules! I'm sick and tired of people telling me to cool it—tell *him* to cool it, *he's* the one causing all the trouble!"

So far only three people had raised objections to expelling him, and there was certainly no rush to join them, but the situation was fraught now for those who wanted him out. The three had considerable weight, and Nathan was yet to be heard from. Everyone was watching him now, though they were all trying to hide it. Very little of any consequence could happen at Farmington without his cooperation— that was becoming more obvious all along—power which he was always the first to say should not exist. Another showdown altogether was in the offing, depending on what he did, and he knew it.

With a display of frustration laced with disgust Phyllis Brodsky got up and headed for the john. And just as she started through the door going out: there Makar was coming in. He put both hands up on the door frame, blocking her exit, informing her with that gesture that the door was being used. She stepped back, out of his way.

And into the dining room he came, wearing his long red velvet robe.

They were all sitting in one half of the room, around the fireplace and the head table. Jerry was talking—he quit in mid-sentence. The whole room fell silent with a crack, as though a gavel had sounded. Like an angry judge entering his court, Makar cut through the middle of them, pulling the string on everyone. He took a chair on the other side of the room, ten feet from the nearest person, and there he sat, hands on knees, his whole person charged, erect, motionless, his black skin and red robes dramatized against the white walls.

All the resentment of Nathan had suddenly disappeared—everyone was glad that he was who he was and that he was there, in charge.

He cleared his throat and made some general remarks about the "problems" they were having.

He did not get far, though—Makar interrupted him. "Anybody got anything to say to me, say it to my face. You know what I mean? I mean, anybody got anything to say to me, say it to my face!"

Only a few people were able to look at him—the rest were staring out the windows or at the floor; they could not even look at one another.

"I'll tell you what happened," Makar said. "You want to know what happened, you all have a secret meeting and want to know what happened, but you ain't got nobody to tell you. Ain't nobody here to tell you what happened because ain't nobody here that knows. Ain't nobody here that knows! You in here making movies, writing up your own scripts. You want to put me in your movies, you talk to me about putting me in your movies, don't go putting me in your goddamn movies! I'll tell you what happened, you want to know what happened and you listen to him there," he said, pointing at Jerry as though with a gun, "and he ain't going to tell you what happened because he don't know. He come in wanting to turn the water off the stove. I turn the water on I turn the water off, you know what I mean? And that other kid there," he pointed at Charleyboy, "he was writing things on the windows. I was just sitting there, you know what I mean? Just sitting there! I hear a lot of talk about peace, but I don't see no peace. They ain't going to tell you what happened, because they don't *know!*"

He fell silent, going around the room with his eyes, seeing if anybody was ready to take up his challenge.

"I've seen all the movies, you know what I mean? I've seen *all* the movies. I've seen 'Gone With The Wind,' I've seen 'Birth of A Nation,' I've seen em *all.* I'm going to tell you something: you can't get past this." He laid his hand, delicately, with an ironic reverence, on his forearm, indicating his black skin. "You can't get past this. That's where you at. You want to talk about black and white, don't come around talking to me. I'm past that, you know what I mean? I been past it a *long* time. I've *seen* all the movies."

From where Nathan was sitting Charleyboy's red painting of the graveyard, which was hanging on the white wall behind Makar—the exact same red as his robes—appeared to be resting with perfect balance, like a crown, on the man's black head. Nathan's sense of where they were and what was happening slipped sideways, he skated down, through the static: the table, the walls, his body, the bodies of those around him: they seemed so evanescent at the core, as though some final light were working through them toward the dark. He saw Ortega's death in Makar, sitting there in the chair — and he knew that it must be his own.

For a moment the world as he had always known it never did exist. He shuddered, grabbing it back.

"You want to know what's going to happen, but ain't nobody here going to tell you, ain't nobody here that *knows*. I'll tell you what's going to happen. There ain't much this time around that belongs to me, you know what I mean? But what does is *mine*. This is mine," he said, indicating his lap, his whole body. "Don't come trying to sit on my lap and rub my head. You want to know what's going to happen, I'll tell you what's going to happen, same thing's going to happen that happened to my granddaddy and grandmomma in New Or-*leans,* you know what I mean? You're going to get a kettle of lye in your face. You think you know slave, but you don't. And you, junior," he said, pointing at Bobo....

When Makar was done, the young people answered him, rising to speak. One after another they repeated to this face the things they had said earlier.

Until in the middle of it all Makar got up and walked out.

And they were all left sitting there looking at one another. It was as though they had been around a table which had suddenly disappeared. Anger had been replaced by apprehension and suspicion. Everybody was wondering whether anybody's mind had been changed. A lot of them were watching Nathan again, openly now, waiting for his move. And the longer they waited the more fearful some of them became that he was going to side with Makar. Phyllis Brodsky took the floor and said that what they had just witnessed made her more certain than ever that Makar was pathological. If he was not expelled from the community, she was leaving. She believed in Farmington, believed in everything they were trying to do there, and she was convinced that they were now at the crossroads: either they dealt with their problems, or their problems were going to deal with them. A lot of people applauded. Then Bobo took the floor and said that he didn't know whether he believed in Farmington or not because he didn't know *what* they were doing there, only what they *said* they were doing. "But I'll tell you one thing for damn sure" — he addressed this straight at Nathan — "either that bastard leaves or *I* do. I didn't kill the cocksucker because I figured I was among friends who would find a better way to deal with him. I can get my ass beat up in Boston, and at least there I don't have to sit around listening to somebody tell me it's *my* problem!"

Everybody now was staring at Nathan.

All along he had been thinking of the secrets that were being kept—of what would happen if they knew, all these people, that they were *paying* Makar to be there. He longed to have all that out, everything out, but not here, not now, it would only confuse the issues—which sounded, he well knew, like the whole history of those secrets, all secrets. There was something in him that believed he had all this coming.

The look on Meriwether's face frightened him: it said well there you are, buddy, your precious Bobo and your precious Makar—now choose.

His job would have been a lot easier had her smugness angered him, and Bobo's manipulations, but he was a long way from that. There was something in him that wanted to help the young man save face, that feared worse than anything Meriwether's disapproval, however unfair.

David asked for the floor and said that he was terribly distressed to see the kind of polarization that was taking place. He, for one, had been moved by what Makar said, and he wanted time to think it over. "Let's take a break and meet again after lunch or tonight. Makar can't possibly do any more damage to us than we can do to ourselves. We can't let this break up the community."

"The hell he can't!" Rhonda screamed. "Didn't he just beat the shit out of Jerry and Bobo? Can't you *see?!* Don't you understand *any*-thing? We came here to live because we're tired of getting the shit kicked out of us every time we turn around. Live down here with him and then say he can't do any damage! We're supposed to wait around now for a kettle of lye in the face?! You're all a bunch of finks, I knew it all along!" She burst into tears.

"Let's settle it right now!" somebody said.

That got seconded all around.

"If you paid any attention to what he *said,*" Sinclair insisted, "he offered the obvious solution. He said that if we left him alone there wouldn't be any trouble. It seems to me that has been perfectly obvious all along."

"Who the hell's bothering him?" Bobo demanded. "I didn't do a damn thing to him!"

"Nobody's even *talked* to him for weeks," Jerry said.

"What were you doing the other night in the kitchen?" Medders asked.

"He was trying to help us keep from getting asphyxiated!" Suzie said.

And so it went, around and around and back and forth, until they realized that they had been there before, several times already, and they turned to Nathan again, one last time. And waited, impatient now.

"Let's take a vote," Rafe said.

"We can't do it this way," Nathan said.

That stopped everything, cold.

"Can't do what *what* way?" Meriwether demanded.

"We can't expel him. We've got no right to. We can't expel anybody. We've got to all make it together or none of us do."

No one was prepared for that.

"What if it were Toni?" Meriwether wanted to know—loud enough for several people to hear.

He'd kept what he thought of Toni and the projection room crowd strictly to home. He could not believe that Meriwether had said that— *what* was going on? Wanting to throttle her gave way quickly to something approaching panic. She was sleeping with someone else— or at least wanted to. It was all he could do now to keep his mind on the business at hand.

"It's got nothing to do with Makar," he said. "It would be the same no matter who's involved. This place belongs to him as much as it does to me or you or anybody else here."

"What a crock of shit!" Bobo said.

"We're not all going to make it together," Phyllis said. "Either he leaves or I do. Does that mean this place closes down?"

"No," Nathan said. "If you leave, you leave of your own free will. I'm going to do everything I can to keep you from it, but nobody is going to force you to stay or to leave, you or Makar or anybody else."

"If this is as much my place as it is yours, then I'm going to stay here this winter," Bobo said. "Me and Rafe and Toni and Rhonda and—" he threw his arm out and around, including whoever. "What do you say to that, Professor?"

"Nathan," Jerry pleaded, "you're not being fair!"

"Don't confuse the issue," Nathan said to Bobo. "That's a whole other consideration, and you know it."

"All I know is HORSESHIT!" Bobo yelled.

Rhonda bolted up, throwing her chair backwards to the floor, and ran out the door crying, followed almost immediately by Meriwether. And that, in effect, was the end of it. In a few minutes the only people left in the dining room were Nathan, Medders, David, Alan Sinclair, and Joe Lainard—and Nathan was only half there, debating with himself whether or not to follow his wife.

Nothing more was heard of Bobo's threat to leave but Phyllis Brodsky packed up and went back to New York the next day. Which set up a compromise of sorts: Makar moved out of the Barn and up the hill, into her place. Where a psychiatrist lived for half of the summer, in a small room attached to the back of Franklin House, now Makar Atnui Aknada resided.

What the young people said proved true: they had not known what it was like up the hill to live with him. He was there with you all the time, even when you did not see him for days on end. His radio— which no one knew he had when he lived down the hill—was on day and night, whether he was in the room or not, tuned to WINS in New York, news twenty-four hours a day. It was there even when you weren't aware of him, the constant reiteration of social and political event, like a parody of the universal hum. Nathan in particular had a hard time ignoring it. You knew you didn't know what it meant, even when you thought you did. You got the sense sometimes that Makar was the only one who did not pay it any mind.

All his peace marches, his endless talk about Vietnam and the violence of the political mind, and here he was underwriting it in his own
little utopia—not for a minute did she believe that there was any
principle involved in what he had just done. Everybody was so caught
up in all this rhetoric about freedom and egalitarianism and alter-
natives and self-structuring communities that nobody would ever
know what was going on—least of all him. All his condescending
patience, all his craven white liberal guilt and reasonableness and
selflessness, all his sexy little students whining for daddy to come and
bail them out the first time they got into trouble, all his cute little
community of artists who did nothing but lie around and smoke dope
and rap: they could sit there and listen all day to him carry on about
how important, how revolutionary it was for them to support one
another—but not her. Not any longer. Never again was she going to
listen to him tell her sweetie it was for her own good whatever he did,
and the good of them all. Let him talk to Bobo and Phyllis Brodsky
about support now. *Stupid,* and shameless in the bargain—the first
time somebody a little bit hipper came along, a little bit farther out,
goodbye, Bobo! They could sit there for the rest of their stoned lives
and let him manipulate and dominate them with the idea they were
free if that was what they wanted. Sure they were free, right on! Just
like he didn't really want to run things, was only doing it for the good
of mankind. Just like he could claim not to want power, and believe it
himself—he didn't have to want it, he *had* it. Just like he always had
and always would, until somebody more powerful came along and
took it away from him. Some other man. And he could then be vir-
tuous about it all, believing of course that he had never wanted it to

-61-

begin with. Phyllis Brodsky knew what was going on, she had known all along, and of course she was leaving. He thought because they were married he could betray her in front of all those people whenever he wanted to. He could sweetie somebody else for a while. He could go right ahead playing with himself and the rest of them, trying to spice up their dull little academic lives, their shameless middleclass search for something sexy, but *she* wanted *out!*

Late that afternoon she went for a walk by herself, ran into Ellie, and they had a long commiserating talk about what had happened that morning. "Can you believe it," Ellie said, "can you *believe* the doubletalk?" Ellie had always shared Meriwether's worst opinion of Makar, and together they catalogued the outrageous things he had done, and the even more outrageous reactions of much of the community, expressing serious doubts about whether Farmington could now survive. Ellie had a new horror to report: a few days ago she had a sixty-five dollar watch stolen, the last and the worst of a growing list of thieveries. Their shared indignation brought them closer than they had ever been, and Meriwether broke a longstanding code and vented censure of her husband. Despite her confidence in what she felt, she was not altogether comfortable doing that, however—and that fact itself irritated and depressed her. She begged off, with expressions of gratitude and promises to pick up where they left off later—and continued her walk alone.

She ended up at the gorge. Bobo and Rafe and Toni were there with an innertube, skinny dipping. She was in no mood to socialize, especially since they were naked, but she was drawn to watching them. She worked her way up to a flat rock where she could observe comfortably without being seen. Below her Toni was floating in Diana's pool, an interlude of deep still water in the shallow down-hill rush of the stream, like a dark watch on a narrow sparkling band. Her white body, laid out flat in a back float, turned slowly like a second hand, her long hair in a beautiful spread on the surface. A wrinkle of water traced her shape, pulsing like an aura around her. Rafe and Bobo were taking turns riding the innertube down the white water and shooting out into the quiet pool with whoops of laughter. Meriwether was incredulous at their gaiety after what had happened that morning, both irritated and envious, a combination which made her smile at herself. She moved, in spirit, a little toward them—which surprised her.

Her talk with Ellie was turning sour. Desperate to get out of New

York in the summer, Ellie and David found Farmington a godsend, and they thought that Nathan, whatever his failings, was some kind of saint—nothing was going to change that. Ellie, it seemed clear to her now, didn't really know how humiliating men were because she couldn't afford to know. The comfort they offered to one another seemed yet more proof of their impotence, a couple of women wringing their hands and complaining about how abused they were.

Ashamed now of hiding, Meriwether moved out into the open where the swimmers could see her. She felt a little naked herself without her child, vulnerable, but she was done hiding. Done!

She remembered an incident from earlier in the summer. She had been sitting peacefully on the lawn in front of Franklin House with Mason in her lap. Bobo and Rafe came up the road and cut through the yard on their way to the Music Shed. Bobo was naked from the waist up, trailing his blue denim work shirt by the sleeve like a rag. "Mother Mary!" he said in greeting. That was all. And they both passed on by, smiling. She resented being seen that way, but she said nothing, for she couldn't blame him. For years people had been telling her that she looked like a Botticelli maiden, so beautifully thin, blond, delicate and spiritual, and until recently she had been only too pleased to hear it. It had always been such a seductive place to hide, so comfortable in fact, especially since the child, that she hadn't seen it until recently as a hiding place at all.

Toni was the first to see her, then Rafe and Bobo. They smiled and waved. Bobo cupped his hands to his mouth as though he were going to yell something up to her, but he didn't: held it for a moment, then collapsed in a laugh, and waved, as if to say *later*. She was painfully self-conscious now about their nakedness, especially Bobo's. She envied them their freedom with their bodies—she had missed out on so much of her generation! Relieved that they were not asking her to join, she was nonetheless distressed to see that they obviously knew better.

"It's your own fault," she said out loud.

She avoided Nathan all day, even at dinner. And that night, after she put Mason to bed, she went for another walk and did not return until late. When she got back Franklin House was dark except for a light in Nathan's study, quiet except for Makar's radio out back. She got a book and settled into a wicker chair on the sunporch, her legs pulled up underneath her. There was a standing lamp next to the chair; she was in a small tent of light, aware of the sounds that the house was making, ticking, creaking, settling there in the cool darkness. And the sounds outside, crickets, a car on the road every now and then, lights circling the room, a dog down the hill, Nietzsche. And like a big room in which all the other sounds were little: the radio out back, the twenty-four hour news station from New York. It was strange having Makar up there, weird. She had the feeling that something was about to happen.

Sure she was free—as free as you could be having lived your entire life in a trap. Free to go out and get a job—as a secretary, making a third what he made for work that would bore her to distraction in a month, in a week. And as long as it didn't interfere too seriously with taking care of Mason or with her marriage. Free to sleep with other men if she really wanted to—as long as she was willing to lie, or to brutalize Nathan. It was worse than that even: she had so internalized his possessiveness she didn't want another man, never had. Free to walk out on him of course—if she wanted to spend the next fifteen years alone with the child, or with another man who, chances were, would be even worse. Free to live off her inheritance while it lasted—if she could ever believe that that spoke to the problem. The trap was in her, a lot deeper than she wanted to admit.

"What kind of infection?" he had said.

She cringed, remembering that moment. She had wanted to confront him with how his lack of trust made her feel, what it was doing to her, to him, to them—but she had known that it would do no good. It never had. Either she had to reassure him or perpetuate his fears by pretending she didn't know they were there. She resented that. But not simply, for she knew that she would have resented just as much hearing of them from him, more—at least he was trying now to keep them to himself. Nor did she trust wanting to confront him any more. She suspected herself of trying to blame him too simply for her own lack of interest. She had no infection. It was going to take more than a doctor and hot baths to cure her. Embroidering the story had made her feel less bad about telling it, not only a way out of their tight spot then and for times to come, but also, she had discovered, a perfect handle on the creepiness of the place—you couldn't even stay clean! Objectifying so many truths so perfectly it had seemed hardly a lie at all, but a necessary fiction—suddenly she had felt free, launching off in high spirits into an apology for "no shame whatsoever." How was *that* for getting it all together! Some infection indeed, trying to call it love.

She slammed her book down, determined—to do what exactly she didn't know. How could she, she didn't even know what she wanted. Do *any*thing, as long as it was different!

On her way to his office to tell him that she was going to the projection room, she made up her mind to have it out with him if he said a word—but she found him asleep. Slumped over on the desk, his arm bent crazily under him, asleep. Papers everywhere, letters, the grant proposal, lists, memos, manuscripts, portfolios—he was surrounded by ten thousand things calling for his attention. There was a letter from the President of the Board of Trustees of Farmington with a two-page list of things to be done before the annual meeting later in the summer. Another from the Dean at the Massachusetts College of Art where he was Head of the Photography Department, full of budget and staff problems. A tax bill from the town of Farmington, another bill from the insurance, another from the phone company, another from the bank for the interest on the loan. Three letters that he'd written that morning to trustees, filling them in on the finances and the plans for the annual meeting, and more, and more. A piece of Ellie's novel for him to read, a sheaf of poems by somebody Meriwether had never heard of, a movie script by David.... And the paper work was only a small part of it: there were the broken toilets, the hurt feelings, the phone calls, the visitors, the electrical failures, the trouble with cats in the kitchen, the ambitions, the unending public relations, old Farmingtonites with their often exaggerated claims on the place and the prospective new ones, the town, the churches, the civic groups, the hip dudes in their vans dropping by for a look around, and on and on. He was father to half the young people there and confidant to many of the grownups; and on top of it all his own work, the burden of not getting it done. Staggering, the job he was doing, even to her it was overwhelming—and she thought she knew. Anyone else would have been undone by it all, but he remained gentle and thoughtful, his patience was monumental. He was keeping the place going so that the rest of them, herself included now, could have a good time. Farmington depended on him, and the world everywhere depended on his kind. He had raised being a husband up into husbandry. And what did he get for it but grief, hassle from every side. At the meetings all anybody wanted to talk about was Why They Were There and the Meaning of Farmington and the Necessity of Turning It Into A Permanent Community—and then they would badmouth him for reminding them that they could not handle the debts they already had.

Something in her still wanted to blame him. He probably wouldn't let her pay those bills even if she wanted to (which suddenly struck her as what to do: sell some stock and really *join* the community).

But then she discovered in his journal a record he was keeping of her menstrual cycle: for years he had been noting the day of the month and week on which each of her periods began and ended. And she was overwhelmed with pity. The recent months, many of them, had question marks next to one or another of the dates, some months had no dates at all. She couldn't blame him for anything.

She uncrooked his arm, and tried to lift him up so that he would be more comfortable. But he was too heavy for her to do much with.

Something very strange happened to her when she was trying to lift him. It reminded her of a dream that she had had the night before. She thought for a moment that she was going to remember it: she had the feel of it, the whole thing seemed to be hovering there on the blind side, within reach, it had to do with...what? For a moment she thought she was going to catch it. But then it was gone, without a trace, leaving her struggling...without even a clue....

If she went down to the projection room, she would probably add to his burdens.

If she didn't, she would probably do the same thing.

Was that what being a grownup was all about?

She shuddered involuntarily.

For a long time she just stood there at the desk beside her husband, her eyes glazed, her mind a blank. Then she turned slowly and mounted the stairs and turned off the light and took off her clothes and climbed into bed and pulled the covers over her head.

And then suddenly threw them off, shuddering again, and dressed hurriedly.

She left a note for Nathan saying she had gone out for a walk.

Once outside she felt better.

Her determination began to desert her, however, the minute she went out the door: it was like walking into a cave: she could not see a thing. She stood for a while a few steps out into the yard, unable to believe how dark it was.

She could barely see her own body.

Makar's radio was playing out back.

Finally she went ahead, feeling her way slowly out to the road, a step at a time. She would find Bobo and persuade him not to leave.

At Van Velder they told her to check the projection room—which was what she was afraid of. She had never been there this late. But she went ahead, picking her way cautiously up the dark hillslope toward the Barn. Spooky was what it was. She stopped, incredulous all over again at the darkness—she could barely make out the building, thirty yards or so ahead. There were no stars, but there was no evidence of the cloud cover either, it was that dark, the heavens themselves had vanished. On the other side of the lacy sound of the crickets the silence seemed to be expanding, Makar's radio out there on the edge.

As she was standing there, awed and a little frightened by where she was and what she was doing, she became conscious of voices and laughter in the darkness somewhere up ahead of her. At first she thought she was hearing things. She wondered how come, attentive as she had been, she had not heard it before. It was coming from up ahead, just around the corner of the Barn, something very private. It was eerie.

She wanted to go back.

But she went ahead, more slowly, swinging out away from the Barn, keeping her distance. She saw now what appeared to be a concentration of fireflies...in the field next to the Barn...only there were too many of them, and they were too bunched up for fireflies. The only thing she could think of was dope—but she refused to let herself turn back now. Slowly she made her way through the dark toward whatever it was. She could not see any figures, but she could hear laughter —muted, subdued, as though an effort were being made to conceal it....

In the doorway of the projection room a lighted Carousel projector was sitting on a chair, and out there in front of it were these fireflies, all bunched together, dancing in mid-air. It was strange what she was seeing, fundamentally disorienting: there was no sense of scale or distance, those specks of light could have been five feet away or fifty, and there was no sense even of their actuality: it could have disappeared instantaneously and you would have believed that it had never been there.

Finally she figured out what was going on. The Carousel was projecting a crazy-quilt of multi-colored dots of light, and several people were dancing in them—a moving screen! Even after she figured that out, she could not see human shapes or movements. Meriwether sat down, slowly, on the cold ground, hardly aware of what she was doing

—drew her knees up to her chest and watched. If the image had been projected on something stable you could have seen it as an image, or if there were a sufficiently large area of light in the image somewhere you could have seen the dancers as dancers, but the combination destroyed the familiarity of both and gave you something you had never seen before—this utterly strange phenomenon vibrating in a futuristic mid-air. Occasionally a dancer dropped out and another took his place, occasionally the slide changed or someone laughed or someone said something, but mostly it was perfectly quiet, just the whir of the projector there in the dark. She understood now that the voices were muted in reverence, not in hiding. It was as though she had been living all these years with a fishbowl on her head, painted about with horizons and seasons, with rooms and set-piece scenes from life, around and around with little figures of Nathan and Mason, fear, resentment, frustration, tight little people clutching tightly to one another—and abruptly it was off....

When the last slide was shown the projector threw out a cone of white light, and against the tree on the ridge the shadows of the dancers were all of a sudden unearthly tall. Once again Meriwether could hardly believe what she was seeing: those enormous figures dancing across the horizon, why they were the very people dancing right there in front of her, people she knew, people she saw every day! With a laugh she jumped up and running into the light joined them, spinning like a curled leaf in an eddy. The other dancers smiled at her, well look who was here, and she smiled back, look indeed—she had been there all along without knowing where it was!

Meriwether spread her arms and laughed, tall for a change, watching herself dance.

"You could really get addicted to this!" she said to Toni.

"Why not?" Toni said.

She thought about rousing Nathan, to show him what was really going on in this place he thought he was running. But Bobo got her into a dance, and she forgot she even had a husband. Without a word he welcomed her to the projection room, extending his greeting like a hand at the station: and without a word she accepted. Next she danced with Toni, hip to hip, tall on the ridge. Smiles ran down their slender arms like electricity, crackled in the night air like snapping fingers.

Astonished she was that it seemed to make no difference to anyone that she had never been there before. All they seemed to care about was that she was there now—that was all it took to get in, simply wanting to. And she was made to feel free to leave whenever she wished, to come back or not as she saw fit. Astonished and humbled, for she knew that she herself had never been that generous, that open.

Later, Bobo walked her up the hill, and they stopped in the graveyard, sat with their backs to tombstones and talked. She was amazed by how different he was now from the loud foul-mouthed kid, which was all she had ever seen of him, and she told him that, and told him that she had come down there tonight to find him and ask him not to leave. Soon it came out that he could not go anywhere without Nathan's approval—except back to the hospital.

"Nathan?!"

"I thought you knew."

"Knew *what?* Nathan's got *custody* of you?!"

She was furious all over again. She knew in her bones how Bobo must be feeling. His threat to leave had been impotent—just as her own thoughts of leaving were—and Nathan had known it all along. He had humiliated them, all right, in more ways than she had known.

Bobo was telling her about the day he had been released. He had cut his hair, from halfway down his back to up above his ears, he had shaved, he had convinced the doctor and then he had convinced his mother and father.... As the day drew nearer he grew more and more afraid, terrified actually that something would go wrong. The night before he couldn't sleep. He got up at six and polished his boots, clipped his fingernails, took a bath, put on a suit and tie and sat on the edge of the bed and waited, sure that Farmington had folded or his parents had reneged. Finally the orderly came, forty-five minutes late, and led him out into the carpeted reception room. He embraced his mother, hands to elbows, and she extended her cheek for him to kiss, talcum and rouge. He shook hands with his father. They looked him up and down, the hair, the suit and tie, he thought for a moment he was going to get their approval, but his mother's eyes fixed on his boots, and then his father's.

"You're not going to wear those things, are you?" his mother demanded.

"Mother!" he pleaded. He had agreed to be treated as though he were crazy in order to stay out of jail, and he had agreed to act out his mother and father's idea of sanity in order to get out of the hospital, and still it was not enough. "It's all I've got!"

"All you want to do is humiliate us," she said. "You're still sick. The doctor said you were still sick. All you want to do is humiliate us.!"

Meriwether reached out and took Bobo's hand.

"They've got you, and they never let you forget it," Bobo said. "All they know how to do is rub your face in their shit."

The sky had cleared: a three-quarter moon.

"Sergeant Pepper" was on the stereo at Van Velder. All around them in the graveyard were tiny American flags, and plastic flowers. The seat of Bobo's worn-out Levis—he was lying on his stomach now, stretched out beside her, propped on his elbow, a blade of grass between his teeth—was patched with an American flag.

She did not try to talk, just held his hand and shut her eyes and squeezed.

Why hadn't Nathan told her? She felt betrayed. What was going on?

She knew why he hadn't told her. Custody was exactly what he wanted, of everybody—but he didn't want to admit it.

A plane passed overhead, on its descent into Hartford, the wing lights like a coupled pair of shooting stars.

She remembered a sequence of pornographic pictures she had seen recently, one in particular, early on in the story, of the man and woman sitting fully clothed in the back seat of a cab, his hand between her legs, her hand pressed gently on the bulge in his pants.... And that reminded her of another picture, this one from an entirely different context, a fine line drawing, of a naked woman on her knees, her legs spread, seen from behind, her genitals drawn with a powerfully hypnotic realism. There was something scary about it, she would have bet anything it had been drawn by a man....

When she came back to Bobo and the graveyard she discovered with a jolt that he was telling her how he had spent most of his life trying to convince his mother that pornography ought to be legalized—a real jolt, for she had made no mention of what she was thinking.

"Momma would say, 'You're talking about those *stag* films and those dirty pictures?!' and I'd say, Right on, Momma! and she said, 'Well we might as well go ahead and invite our children into the bedroom!' and I said, So *that's* what's going on in your bedroom, no wonder you don't want it legalized!"

They laughed, Meriwether and Bobo.

She wanted to tell him about Nathan, the real Nathan. How he couldn't buy gasoline for the car without knowing the lead content, so that he could figure out not just the pollution but the price per gallon against the long term effect on the muffler. To tell him that a couple of days ago she had gone into the kitchen at Franklin to find pinned up on the cupboard a xeroxed *Consumer Reports* list of all the breakfast cereals ranked according to their nutritional value; that he couldn't park the car without figuring out the best way to park it, which usually had to do with how fast it could be got out in case of an emergency; that he knew the comparative prices of every standard item in every grocery store in Cambridge within reach, and had a pretty good idea, on any given shopping day, whether it would pay to go to more than one—and he didn't even do the shopping; that if he didn't have the same amount of the same bourbon from the same glass every night at the same time before he went to bed, he would find it hard to fall asleep; that he was scared of what was going on down there in the projection room, scared of dope, scared of Toni. She wanted to tell him that all that super-father stuff was not the whole story, not by a lot, that she wasn't simply the mother and housewife she appeared to be. But she could not talk about her husband. She told him instead how she had wanted to hide that afternoon at the gorge for fear they would ask her to skinny dip with them.

He smiled, and squeezed her hand.

Part of her was standing off to the side and watching them in horror, her of all people! and him! but there was another part off to the other side applauding, finally! and yet another right in the middle, concerned not with the meaning of what was happening but responsive simply to the fact that it felt good to be with him, that in fact she hadn't felt so good for a long time.

The Rolling Stones were on now, " Jumping Jack Flash."

When it came time for them to leave, he kissed her foot, and when she smiled he took her big toe, momentarily, in his mouth.

As soon as Toni got up from her mattress after the next yoga class and went to the coffee pot in the corner—switching on the table lamp that sat on the floor next to it, as she always did—Meriwhether knew without being told that this time she was fixing a cup for each of them. She had not known for sure until then that she was going to stay on. Waiting on the hillslope below the Barn, she watched a few minutes later as the other woman made her way carefully down to her, balancing two cups of coffee against a cat on her shoulder. All along Meriwether had been thinking that Toni McHugh lacked something —she could do the grand thing but not the small—she lacked intimacy (which seemed fair enough, not so much a price to pay as a bargain). But that view of her changed, beginning that night over coffee. Toni did not lack intimacy so much as she redefined it. In the weeks to come there was nothing they did not talk about there on the hillside after class, but even the most private subjects seemed in Toni's presence somehow impersonal. That turned out to be not the horror Meriwether had always thought it was, but—she should have known —clear-headedness. It always made her feel good to be around Toni.

"What should I do?" Meriwether would ask.

Toni would never answer.

In her presence Meriwether was forever discovering that she felt something. And that it was never quite what she thought she was feeling. She really couldn't stand to be around Nathan at times now, that's what she really felt. And painful and frightening as that was, she was excited to be feeling it. With each new discovery she would go through a period in which she was more interested the clearer it got— then in Toni's presence that would turn around. So she felt guilty about having money—so what? Toni made her feel free.

"Do something about it or quit complaining?" Meriwether asked to have that confirmed.

"I didn't say that."

"Well what did you mean when you said sex was private money and money was public sex?"

"I meant I wouldn't dream of telling anybody what to do with their marriage or their money."

"You're *not* saying deal with it or quit complaining?"

"I'm not saying anything. I'm listening."

"But you got me to say it, didn't you?"

Toni shook her head and laughed.

She was, Meriwether saw, absolutely practical. For all the cosmic dance she was the most matter-of-fact person Meriwether had ever encountered. Whenever anyone talked about how far-out the meditations were she told them they were missing the point. Whenever Meriwether talked about freedom, Toni got it around to hammers and nails. When chaos was accepted, with Dylan cited as the authority—a theme song for some at Farmington—she shrugged and walked away. "Chaos on a hundred dollars a day," she called it, "anarchy on Mastercharge." She wasn't uninterested in what was going on between Meriwether and Bobo—she wasn't uninterested in anything—but there was a limit to how seriously she could take it. A professor's wife having her first affair with one of her husband's former students, in secret—the "who's-fucking-who movie" she called it. In a passing remark she could snatch Meriwether to the ground, show her her own feet and how to keep them planted firmly—which, given the turn her life was taking, was exactly what she needed. She wanted nothing to do with what Toni called the "psycho-sexual melodrama" of Farmington, and she was grateful for a friend who could tell her and keep telling her the ins and outs of the script. Toni laughed at the notion of being apolitical, "a leisure of the theory class," believing that the very idea was a chimera. Her relationship with Rafe seemed to have little to do with sex or affection, even at first, after a while nothing. She was with him because they shared a vision—the projection room wasn't it, the projection room was on the way to it, a kind of basic training. Toni was a lot more political than Meriwether was at first prepared to understand. On the other side of the slide shows was street theater. She did not want the war stopped—she wanted the war brought home, with a vengeance. Although Makar was the most interesting person there, she said, he was "badly crippled—he thinks his feelings are more important than they are." Meriwether said that he certainly had come to the right place; she herself was guilty of the same thing. Toni looked at her as if to say yes that was indeed true—so? It wasn't a challenge or a dismissal, it was a simple question, a lot simpler than Meriwether was used to. It was the revolutionary in Toni that redefined intimacy. She made Meriwether feel free of herself: aware as she had never been before of the many things more important than her feelings.

Even when those glasses weren't perched on top of her head they were part of what Meriwether saw in the quick turns of Toni's head, the steadiness of her gaze. They caught something of her alertness, like a cat's ears. She was always listening. There was nothing between you and her eyes, nothing between her and what they were looking at. You had the feeling that she knew what was going on around her, all around her. She seemed always ready to laugh, holding back in order to maintain her attention. Nothing about her blinked. There on the hillside late at night, a few feet from the Wish Hole, Meriwether many times could not look directly back. Hurtling toward some Y in the road, her eyes couldn't choose, and when she did she felt herself divided, two half-selves going off in different directions. Try as she did to straighten herself out, she stayed out of register, displaced off to the side of Toni's stare. The large blue-grey eyes were there, in the middle of what Meriwether was trying to look at, unblinking, but it was as though she were looking at them around a corner. She felt cross-eyed

—it was exhausting. Toni was not telling her to stop lying to Nathan —she was not telling her anything. At such times Meriwether felt vaguely nauseated. She had wanted another grown-up around—she figured now she had one.

Nathan was fascinated with Makar's claim to know all the movies. For years he had wanted to work in film, and now, with David there to learn from, with his photography at a stand still, with collaborations the order of the day, he was teased by the idea of doing a film with Makar. If the black man knew all the movies, maybe he knew the Farmington movie, and maybe, if the approach were canny enough, they could make it together.

One thing that held him back was professional vanity. He did not want to serve another apprenticeship, especially not while he was director of the community, especially not in front of Toni McHugh. Another was fear of presumption. He had no idea what Makar thought of him as an artist—if he thought anything, which he probably did not. Despite his reservations—and, once he decided they were unworthy, *because* of them—he made up his mind to broach the idea of a collaboration; he was waiting for the right occasion, when it fell right into his lap.

Through a colleague in Boston he found out that the University of Chicago was looking for a last-minute replacement in their Black Studies program, and he arranged for Makar to fly out for an interview. On the way to the airport he explained his idea. He would set up a movie camera inside the painting studio looking at the open door. One after another several members of the community, chosen by Makar, would walk across the bright sunlit lawn, through the door into the studio, and address the camera—that was the opening scene. Makar himself, the last one in, would close the door—on the back of which, running from bottom to top, the word TIME was written with spray-paint in large black letters, a relic from a previous summer. And then, in the assembled presence of those he had sent in before him, against the backdrop of a large TIME stood up on its T, Makar could do whatever he wanted to do, direct his own Farmington Movie.

"Un-huh," Makar said. "I see what you're saying. Flight 112 leaves at 2:05 p.m., and you're paying the fare? Is that what you're saying? Line a bunch up at the door, run em in, and then fly?"

Nathan hesitated, unable to believe for a moment that he understood, but he did, or thought he did. He laughed. "Okay. Sort of. Yeah!"

"Flight 112, 2:05 p.m., July 12, 1969? So they say?"

"Right! TWA!"

"I thought you was saying American."

"Actually it's TWA, but it might as well be American. Same thing."

"What you're saying is, a man in his TIME don't confuse actuality with reality? Is that what you're saying?"

"Now that you mention it," Nathan said, "I might as well be!"

"Un-huh. Now. That I mention It. You might as well Be? Un-huh. You might. But then you might not. I was thinking about Mississippi mud."

Nathan did not know what to do with that one, but he was heady now, wanted badly to keep up. "You mean the flight might get transferred to Delta?"

"Delta who?"

"Mississippi mud."

"M-i-ss-i-ss-i-pp-i," Makar sing-songed.

"What's Mississippi mud?"

"Mud in Mississippi, I reckon," Makar said.

By the time they got to the airport Nathan was high on Makar's presence. The terminal itelf was an extended trope, a stage on which rituals of arrival and departure were being conducted, in which numbers played some portentous role. The planes themselves, taking off and landing, were seen now in all their improbability, their flight both exhilarating and frightening, as though the whole business of the place were not work-a-day transportation at all but some extraordinary challenge to man's place in the scheme of things. A terminal indeed! All those perfectly ordinary people—*flying!* While Makar was checking his bag, Nathan played roulette with a rack of inspirational literature, and there, spinning through the middle of all the Christian titles, was a book called *The Negative Power of Positive Thinking*—as if Makar's presence had conjured it. All the way back to Farmington he was intrigued with that title, and with the fact that the more he thought about it the less sense it made.

When Makar returned Nathan was at the airport to meet him, eager to find out whether they were going to make a film together. But it was obvious from the minute the man walked through the door that they were not going to pick up where they had left off, not then anyway. On the surface Makar was pleasant enough, but he was elsewhere, and he made it clear that Nathan was not supposed to come looking for him. If it had been anyone else, you would have assumed that something untoward had happened in Chicago—which in fact was the case, the Blacks there had no use for him at all—but Nathan, beyond making any assumptions about Makar whatsoever, read his inaccessibility as just Makar, one of him anyway.

A few days later, after a long talk with David, who got him excited again about making a film, Nathan went to Makar's room looking for him. The radio was playing, and the minute Nathan was close enough to hear he realized how fragile his sense of well-being was—found himself in a bind. The radio did not mean that Makar was there, but if he went on in now and Makar *was* there he would find himself caught between the news and the black man, neither of which he could handle with half a mind. So he hung back, out of sight, caught in the news, listening for Vietnam. It was a good thing he did too, for there was a report out of Washington which he needed time and privacy to assimilate, new talk of Red China entering the war. He checked his watch, slipped away from Makar's door, back into the house, got his transistor, closed the door to his office and sat down to wait for NBC News on the Hour. (He did not trust WINS—or more exactly he did not know the New York station well enough to trust it or not; with NBC, and to a lesser extent CBS, he knew all the commentators, how to weight what they said and how they said it, knew their voices, their sources, their biases and predilections.) As the hour approached he grew anxious that someone would interrupt, which would put him in another bind, for he hated for anyone to see how obsessed he was with those five minute reports, even Meriwether—so he took the transistor and went for a short walk up the road. After the news was over he got himself a cup of coffee and a cigarette (one of the five he allowed himself each day, except in emergencies), and sat alone on the sun-porch working his way through the first phase of the anxiety.

Had he gone on into Makar's room he would have found Toni and

Rafe being held prisoner there, and while it is hard to imagine exactly where things would have gone from there, the course of the rest of the summer probably would have been altered, and the course of several lives. They were both sitting on the floor with their backs to the wall, heads laid back in exhaustion, their eyes open for fear of closing them. Makar was between them and the door, where he had been for hours, sitting straight in a straight-backed chair, his shirt off and his large eyes shut, barefoot, much the same figure he presented in the Chesterfield Community Church. He may have been asleep, he may have been asleep most of the time, there was no telling—they were not about to try to find out. The radio had been playing the entire time, the same news over and over and over again, hour after hour, an analogue to their imprisonment, at once tedious and nightmarish. At one point Toni tried to sleep, trusting Rafe to stay alert—only to wake up, suddenly, both at the same instant, with Makar hovering over them, staring. A hand gun in a holster hung on a nail next to the door. They had come with respect, to ask him for his influence, specifically with Nathan, and they had been greeted with ridicule. "Un-huh. Un-huh. The big take-over. I'll show you take over. I'll show you slave." They could smell him, and it was not any smell they knew, not sweat, not dope, not feet, not black, nothing they recognized, neither pleasant nor particularly foul, a kind of sweet and sour musk that emanated from him, like everything else. He did not come at them with words or looks or any of those off-balance moves he used on the outside: he just sat there, most of the time with his eyes closed, coming off himself, surrounded by it, whatever it was: as though he had himself under a power lens, the pores magnified, the mouth, the eyes: everything about him eerie, uncannily large and clearly defined: as though he were hallucinating himself, emerging through his swollen mouth and bulging eyes: as though parts of him had a life unto themselves, were giving birth to it there in the tight dark room. It was as though there were more than one of him. All night they assumed that he would let them go when it got light, but it had been light for a long time now, it was getting on toward lunch. If there was anyone around who could be depended upon not to freak out or try to pass it off as a bad trip, who was not intimidated by Makar, it was Nathan. Ordinarily he was the last person in the community either of them wanted to see, but there were times now when both were longing privately for him. Perhaps that was one of the influences that brought him so close to the door— for indeed it was his presence there that seemed to set them free, a less dramatic rescue than they were fantasizing, but far safer. When Nathan stopped in the bushes there outside the door, listening for a moment to the news, Makar opened his eyes and stared at the wall as though he knew something were going on. And a moment later, as abruptly and mysteriously as the whole thing started, he was gone without a word, leaving them finally to themselves.

When Nathan returned, nobody was there, though nothing seemed changed to him, the radio still on, the door still half open. He stood several feet back, so as not to violate the room's privacy, and called Makar's name. There was no answer. Just the news on the radio. And Jerry playing *Pierot Lunaire* in the hexagon up the hill. He called again, a little louder this time. Still no answer. He waited a moment longer, then climbed the makeshift steps and slapped on the door with the flat of his hand, loud. "Makar?" And then finally stepped cautiously, hesitantly into the dark room. It was only the third time since Makar had moved that he had been in there, and the first time alone—which he was not at all sure he should be doing. What he hoped to accomplish with Makar not there he did not know.

The room was full of presences, teeming. He walked right into the middle of them, like a mess of spider-webs—flinched, shivered, grabbing at himself, trying to shake them off. He knew that it was not the news this time, that it was not really the news last time, that it was never the news—but still. . . .

He did not dare touch the radio, dare touch anything.

So there he stood, immobilized in the middle of Makar's small windowless room: caught again—by what this time he had no idea: held.

Then he saw the gun hanging on the wall, the shoulder holster, darkened with sweat, hanging on a nail next to the door.

And everything snapped into place.

He smiled.

All those amorphous fears went straight to the gun, like metal shavings to a magnet—found a shape there, a story, something he could take hold of.

He knew immediately that the gun had to go, and that if Makar was not willing to get rid of it then he would get rid of Makar.

Moving now with a great slow sensuousness, as though he and everything in the room were in a dream, Nathan took the holster and the gun off the wall and sat down where Makar had sat all night holding Toni and Rafe prisoner—lowered himself into the chair the way Makar lowered himself into the preacher's chair at Chesterfield, and with a smile folded his hands carefully, almost lovingly, over the gun in his lap.

He waited.

He was excited, more excited than he had been in a long time. Profoundly excited.

Jerry was still playing his piano in the practice shed up the hill, the sound of Schoenberg coming and going in the interstices of the news.

Nathan shut his eyes, trying to calm himself.

More and more with each move now he came to look like Makar. It was as though the black man were working on him through the gun, through the chair, through the room—as though Makar were already there, had perhaps been there all along, were making his appearance now. Nathan thought he was concentrating on Makar, but it was as though Makar were concentrating on him. At the very moment when he felt most alive, most substantial and in control, it was as though he were disappearing, as though Makar were taking his place, coming into the room through him.

Nathan was at the top of himself, keyed, ready to deal, when Makar stepped up out of the sunlight into the darkened room. He rose quickly from the chair, moved back to keep his distance, and held the gun up by the shoulder strap.

"You can't have this here," he said.

He started to apologize and explain—but he stopped himself.

He could not see Makar's face: just a silhouette standing there in the doorway.

"I beg your pardon?"

It was not Makar's voice. Nathan experienced a moment of uncertainty, a lightheadedness that made him reach for the back of the chair.

The figure in front of him was unmistakably that of Makar, but for a moment he thought it must be somebody else.

"I don't know what you're doing with it, and I don't want to know, but it's got to go. Right now."

As his eyes adjusted he saw Makar's face emerge from the shadows. Or more exactly he saw his eyes and his mouth come forth: those great protuberant eyes: the enormous mouth: they emerged from deep within the shape of his head like the visage of a frog in a dark well. And then suddenly it was even more strange than that: the eyes disappeared: as if they had gone back under: and it was just the mouth looking at him, those great mucocutaneous lips, black skin swollen to the revelation of its raw red undersides, like a whole thing breathing and staring at him. For a moment Nathan was in a kind of tunnel: he was at one end and Makar's mouth at the other: an eerie pressure building up all around, as though they were under water, and there swimming suddenly out of the darkness toward him, right up in his face, was this raw bold creature in the form of a mouth.

"Un-huh. Un-huh."

It was Makar's voice again.

It said, "I see what you mean."

For several seconds then neither of them spoke: they were staring at one another: the space between them contracted, though neither moved.

"Un-huh. Just what did you have in mind doing with it?"

"I don't care," Nathan said. "Just get rid of it, right now. I want it out of here, right now."

"Un-huh. I reckon I could... pawn it, is that what you're saying? In terms of saying I could pawn it?"

There was an accusation of racism in Makar's remark, and Nathan was tempted to try to answer it, but he did not know how. "I really don't care what you do with it as long as you get it out of here."

"Or I reckon I could wrap it up in a little box and mail it to momma down in Lexington."

"That's fine."

"Naw it ain't," Makar said.

"Why not?"

"Momma's dead."

"I don't care what you do with it, just get it out of here, right now."

"Or I reckon you could take it."

"I don't want it. I don't want any guns around here."

"I reckon you could sleep with it under your pillow and nobody could get a-holt of it." He chuckled. "Cept Miss Murwether. That's her name, ain't it, Miss Mur-wether?"

Nathan refused to answer that.

"You mean you ain't sleeping with Miss Mur-wether no more?"

"Shut up, Makar!" Nathan said. "We're talking about the *gun*!"

"Is that what we're talking about?"

"Yes it is."

"Is this here the movie you was wanting to make with me?"

"No, it's not. This is the last thing in the world I wanted to happen."

"I thought you came in here to talk about making a movie."

"That happens to be true, yes, but we're going to have to deal with this first."

"The movie where you come into my room when I'm not there?"

"I'm sorry about that, but let's not change the subject, okay?"

"You know what happens in that movie, don't you? I take the gun away from you."

"Let's not play games!"

"You standing in my room with my gun telling me what I got to do with it—how we going to get around playing games?"

"By getting rid of the gun," Nathan said.

"When it's your rules, it ain't a game, huh. This what you been doing all them push-ups for? Running of a morning? Get yourself all powered up? Don't you reckon I could take that gun away from you if I wanted to?"

"No," Nathan said flatly, "you couldn't."

Makar chuckled. "I reckon I see what you mean. In terms of saying, put a gun in a man's hand and he gets crazy? Is that what you're saying? Make him forget who he is and what's happening? Make him think he can do things he can't do? I reckon I see what you mean. Can't have nothing like that around here. Is that what you mean?"

"That's exactly what I mean."

"You know what I'm going to do with that gun when I take it away from you? Gonna make you eat it. That's one way of getting rid of it, ain't it? You ever eat gun? Put the barrel in your mouth and put your tongue in the barrel?" He puckered his swollen lips and pushed his whole face abruptly forward, working his mouth like an ape's—as though he knew exactly what Nathan had seen a moment ago in the tunnel and was mocking it. "I knew a fellow once that used to fuck himself in the ass with a loaded gun. Called it rushin roué. You know rushin roué?"

"Let's deal with the gun, Makar."

"I didn't reckon you did," he said, and chuckled. Then, looking him in the eyes, "We dealing, we dealing."

"Let's take it into Northampton right now and sell it."

"We got better movies to make than fightin' over an old gun—is that what you're saying?"

"Yes, we do," Nathan said.

Makar was staring at him. They were quickly now approaching some juncture. Neither of them said anything for what seemed like a long time. The radio was getting on Nathan's nerves again, but he refused to be stared down. Finally Makar conceded, and they relaxed a little.

Conceded exactly what, though, Nathan was not sure.

"I reckon we could go up and throw it in the creek."

"That's fine with me," Nathan said. For the first time he sensed the possibility that Makar would permit what he was saying to be taken at face value. "Let's go!"

And sure enough, he did. On the way up to the gorge Nathan thought that the worst of it was probably over, and his mind eased a little. He was proud of himself—so proud, in fact, that he had to keep telling himself how foolish that could be. This was the first time he had ever talked to Makar that way, and he was thinking that perhaps there was a lesson in it.

When they got to Diana's Pool they sat down together on a large flat rock near the water. He still had the gun, but he was uncomfortable with it now, as though continuing to hold on to it were insulting to Makar—so, wrapping the shoulder strap neatly around the holster, he put it down on the rock between them.

And immediately wished that he had not.

But there it was.

An elm leaf, curled in on itself like a conch, drifted down the stream past them; it was standing up in the water, as though its base were weighted. It looked like a sea horse, or the Horsehead Nebula. It bobbed along, spinning slowly, working its head proudly like a five-gaited champion. "Look!" Nathan said, and pointed, and Makar said "Un-huh!" and together they watched it prance slowly past them, turning this way and that, and on into a slow eddy a few yards downstream. There was another leaf under the same influence, a larger flat one, a maple. It followed the horsehead on into the eddy, rose out high behind him on the first turn, specks of sunlight on the water like stars in a surrounding galaxy. They turned their backs on one another, spinning through a full circle, then turned to face again, circling more slowly this time: the horsehead bowed and the flat maple curtsied: they came close: and then backed off again.

"That must be his fair lady," Makar said.

Everything they did now, the two leaves, was a dance. The fair lady meandered off, playing hard to get; and the horsehead had a one-night stand with another leaf, which sent her into a momentary spin; but she recovered her dignity and wandered off, pretending not even to notice.

Nathan was fetched up: with delight he watched, his elbows on his knees, so intent on the performance that it was a while registering with him that it was not Makar who spoke those words.

That must be his fair lady.

Nathan heard the words again in his head, the tone, the pronunciation — unmistakably not Makar. It was a white man's voice, the same one he had heard earlier. One minute he was being thoroughly charmed by the leaves, the next he was.... He had not the slightest idea now what he was afraid of, certainly not the gun any longer, or even Makar, or not simply Makar. He kept telling himself that perhaps he mis-heard, that the stress had gotten to him. He wanted to look at Makar, to see for himself what was going on over there — but he stared at the water, no longer seeing anything. He was waiting.

And Makar, as though he had been waiting for him to hear and waiting for him to wait, told him then a story — or more exactly continued the story he had been telling him all along....

"God knows if there had been another place in all that fetid neighborhood to get a cup of coffee after eight o'clock in the evening, I never would have gone back. I *knew* the minute I sat down that she would... well, excuse me, I have no heart for this, really. The minute you say *she* you know what is in store. If not this week, then the next, or the next. It loves to happen. The Tottle House it was called, as I remember. I was no child, God knows. Not that I ever was. I had, supposedly, spent several long years already in the service of my country. What I was doing in Lexington remains to this day a mystery, though surely it had something to do with my dear brother who was determined to live there, because of his wife I think. Wherever, whenever determination is involved there is always a wife in it somewhere, always. The military is much maligned, and it shouldn't be, there are worse things in this world. Several years and no small expense of spirit, much of it in the Caribbean. In Communications, as they say. I had, on entering the Tottle House, read only five things in my entire life, but I had selected them with great cunning, and in fact parlayed them more than once into a reputation for vast learning. When I saw her reading *Death In Venice* I knew that she would break my poor back, probably before morning. *The Brothers K* perhaps, or even *Ulysses* or *The Tempest*, but *Death In Venice* — what can one say? Lie there, my art — indeed. Her name, you won't believe this, was Shelley, and she was, by her own confession, a student at the University and a lover of horses and dulcimers. Aren't we all. I had no more gotten to bed that very night than she was at the door. Carrying her books under her hooded rain-coat. She said, as I remember, standing there on the porch with her books under her hooded raincoat, that she had come over so that *I* could fix *her* a cup of coffee. I was neither a student at the university nor…"

Nathan's body went off on its own, did not trust him with what was happening—it listened as though memorizing, every word, every into-nation and inflection—

"…nor a lover of horses and dulcimers, but that seemed to mean very little to the young lady. She was putting herself through school by serving coffee at night, and chocolate icebox pie, which was infinitely more than I could say for myself, and I'm sure that if I saw her again today I would be moved all over again to tears. I fucked her on the basin in the bathroom, and had to watch myself in the mirror the whole time. Which served me right, as I always do. It loves to happen. Once you start something like that there is absolutely no way to stop. She would have had me believe, along with her, that all the world's universities and dulcimers had been mere preparations for our meet-ing, which of course I did, and which of course they probably were. We managed, in our extremity, to turn the water on in the basin, which she made much of in her poems. She was determined to talk afterwards. There was nothing I could do, there was nothing either of us could do, there never is. And she was still there the next morning, curled up beside me with her arm across my chest and her raincoat in the middle of the floor. There was no way to get out of bed without waking her. She was, of course, having a love affair with her writing teacher, who became terribly jealous and wanted to send all five of my poems to Karl Shapiro at *Poetry* magazine. And I had been in town only three weeks. I apologized to everyone incessantly, offered to join the Navy again, anything, but they insisted. I was flattered, of course, and wrote three pages of a novel. The one unforgivable thing about decent people is that they insist. They wanted to meet their class at my place. He was one of the three decent men I have ever known, a fool of course and a teacher of writing, surrounded by young women named Shelley, I owed him nothing, but I will never forgive myself. We sat there all on the floor drinking cheap wine from paper cups and listened to her read a story called "Pegasus" which was not, as he and the rest assumed, about him, but about me. He did nothing to deserve that. After these sessions he would take her back to her place and they would do whatever they did before he went home to his wife and children—and then she would come back to my place. She was, the young lady, perhaps the only person I have ever known more vile than I, but then she had the excuse of her age. I often wonder what has happened to her. She is married, to a filmmaker or photographer, I'm sure, or an avant garde composer, and she lives no doubt in an artist colony somewhere, torn between her child and her lost youth. Titilated from time to time, no doubt, by the poetry of Wallace Stevens and Ezra Pound. Aren't we all."

He stopped—

Nathan hung there in the silence, his eyes shut, waiting again, in the dark. It was as though the voice collapsed suddenly in on itself, silence, and kept on collapsing, taking him with it. He did not know where he was. He had forgotten the weapon. He had in effect forgotten everything. He could feel Makar over there moving him around. He was not waiting, he realized: he was being waited for.

When Nathan opened his eyes and turned he found Makar pointing the gun at him. The black man was sitting a few yards away: both arms stretched out straight: elbows planted firmly on his raised knees: holding the weapon with both hands: his chin was lowered: he was motionless: he was sighting down the barrel into Nathan's face.

He started talking again, slowly, in his own voice now, telling him what had happened that night at the Captain's Den. He told it as though it had actually taken place, as though it were taking place again, for the first time—which in a sense it was. Nathan found himself there at the bar with South Mouth, at the pool table, in the parking lot—and he believed that he knew for the first time what was going on. When Makar reported what South Mouth said and did, Nathan reiterated it, sometimes out loud, as though hypnotized he was being coached for a role in a movie—which in a sense he was. "Un-huh, un-huh," Makar said, "where *you* living now?" Right along with South Mouth, Nathan grimaced and held his wrist as though it were broken. He believed that all that was mysterious about Makar now made sense, a black man who had worked undercover, all that was powerful as easily understood as guns and karate chops. He had disappeared again, into another of Makar's fictions: he was already playing the role he was being coached for. In a sense he had written it himself. And already his exhilaration was turning to nausea. He believed that Red China was entering the war, that Meriwether was sleeping with another man. "You was looking for me in the wrong place," Makar was saying. "You got to see what you're doing in this business."

Nathan could no longer tell whether his eyes were open or shut, or which gun was which, and he didn't care—he wobbled for a moment, then toppled over on his side and curled up, drawing his legs to his chest.

The next thing he knew he was on his hands and knees, gasping for breath, staring down into a puddle of vomit. Makar was behind him, his hand on his forehead, holding his head up.

"You all right," Makar was saying, "you all right. We just made a little movie, is all. In terms of saying, eating gun is hard on a man's stomach, you know what I mean? I mean you come around wanting to make a movie, I told you what was going to happen, didn't I? Go fuckin' around with a loaded gun ain't no telling where you get off. Wrap yourself up in a little box, ain't no place to go but momma's. It loves to happen. But what happens to love—is that what you're saying? You got a point there—if that's what you want, you know what I mean? I mean I done told you, momma's dead. You know about dead momma, don't you—now there's your movie. There's your point man's picture show. You all right, you all right. I mean if a point's what you want, go to the point doctor, don't come around bothering me. In terms of saying I ain't going to tickle your ass, like what's-her-name with the dog. Carry a big dog around long enough, bound to end up calling it Nietzsche, don't you reckon? I don't want to hear no more about no revolution. Tell her if she wants to play tickle-ass, do it with the dog. There's your movie now—that's what happens to love. They got the projector, but they ain't got the film, you know what I mean? There's your Farmington movie right there. A whole lot of beginning without no middle in sight, point doctor's speech at the end. I mean you all right, get up now, you all right."

There were times later when Nathan was sure that Makar threw the gun into Diana's Pool, when he thought that he could remember seeing it hit the water and sink, the loop of the shoulder strap going under last. But there were other times when he was not at all sure. He remembered clearly the return: they had gone straight out to the road and walked side by side, step for step, on either side of the dividing stripe. A canary yellow Plymouth convertible came up the hill, and they parted symmetrically to let it pass and then came back together again on the other side in perfect sync—putting the car, Nathan fancied, inside a football. They were then correspondingly tiny, he and this black man, walking down the hill in unison, talking about the film they were going to make: were at the wrong end of a scope, about the size they would be on a 16mm frame. For days that inverted scale stayed with him, playing with the peas on his dinner plate, with Mason and the child's toys, with matches and push pins and people's eyes. Makar was wearing a dashiki that day at the gorge, there was no way he could have slipped the holster on without Nathan seeing, but still he found himself, whenever he was in Makar's room, glancing around for evidence of it. And when he was out running in the morning he found himself—when he wasn't searching for a marijuana crop that he suspected Rafe and Bobo of growing—imagining Makar sitting in the undergrowth somewhere: his arms stretched out straight: elbows planted firmly on his raised knees: holding the gun with both hands: sighting down the barrel and panning with the running figure as though he were making a movie. Whenever he became conscious of a silence, whether out running or in his office or in one of the regular community meetings, Nathan found himself preparing for the sudden explosion of a gun. If Makar was around he would look at him, study him. If not, he would try to imagine where the black man was and what he was doing.

As usual Toni did not say a word at the regular Friday night meeting. She had been having it both ways ever since she got there, and he had half a mind to call her hand. It was not even as though she was staying out of it: she was getting like Makar: the more she played at being on the outside the more space she took up within. There she sat with her back to the wall and her knees drawn up, watching first one person and then another, hiding as usual in attentiveness. If you did not suspect that she thought it was all a crock and wanted you to know that she did, you would think she was fascinated by what was going on —which as far as he was concerned was no different from being bored. They needed help—and she was worse than none at all. He resented the fact that she was thought of as the person who got things done. She wouldn't lift a hand for the place—except of course to take it over. He resented the fact that the projection room was thought of as such a success, that no one wanted to face the price they had paid for it. He resented the fact that he got badmouthed for not getting along with her—it was her place to get along with him, with the *whole* community. Everybody was afraid of her and was trying to call it respect. She could have such high principles because she played only by her own rules. Finally Nathan could not take it any longer. At a critical point in the discussion he turned to her and asked her what she thought—less a question than a challenge.

The room fell silent with anticipation. And with some dread. Even those who were always lobbying for showdowns sensed that no good was going to come of this one.

Toni McHugh lifted her head. And smiled. And wet her lips. She was taking a moment, it would seem, to figure out exactly how she wanted to put it.

Meriwether shut her eyes and slid down in her seat.

Toni answered him all right. She said that she found it difficult to take these meetings seriously because they seemed to her to act out Farmington's refusal to take itself seriously. Or even to understand what was involved, what they were—supposedly—doing there. Farmington was part of a revolution whether they liked it or not, she said, they were all part of it, whether they wanted to be or not, the whole country was; and while they all seemed to want to be associated with the excitement of it, few of them seemed to realize what it was all about. Although she was not interested in living there year round herself, she said, it seemed to her that the idea of a permanent community was the only serious topic of discussion. If they were not willing to change their lives, then everything else they were doing there was a lie, or just another summer vacation. "I came here because this place advertised itself as a self-structuring community. All I've seen so far is Camp Farmington."

"Right on!" Bobo said.

It was the truth, clearly seen and stated. And everyone in the room knew it, at least for a few seconds. She was not saying anything that had not been said before—Nathan himself, in fact, had said some of the same things—but it was as though no one had ever heard them before.

Everybody was talking at once.

For a moment there the situation belonged to her.

Makar was sitting in the rocking chair sipping tea, chuckling now and then, but as usual not saying a word. As the room began to fill up with Toni McHugh he stopped rocking and took up watching, very carefully watching what was happening—something that everyone became more or less aware of. At the same time that she was flying about the room from one person to the next, setting them spine straight, leaning them forward into Camp Farmington indeed—roast Lyndon Johnson, not marshmallows!—Makar was commencing to hold the whole thing back a trick, to insinuate himself subtly into what was going on, to put checks of his own on it. Slowly the room's consciousness was drawn toward him, until now, though he had not said a word, people were as aware of him as of Toni and Nathan—expectant, waiting for him to say something, do something.

The word revolution had been used more than usual, which is to say it had been used a lot; Makar began there, calling attention to that fact, indicating several people around the room who had used the word—and finally Toni McHugh.

"And what's-her-name there," he said, pointing his finger at her.

"Don't point," she said.

There was scattered, uneasy laughter as Cupid flew through the air like an arrow, but it died out abruptly—leaving the room polarized around them, electric.

"You know what a revolution is, don't you?" he asked everybody.

No one volunteered.

"No, Makar," Toni said. "We don't know what a revolution is— we're waiting for you to tell us."

"A revolution is three hundred and sixty de-grees," he said. And chuckled.

Several people laughed, quietly, and then, as his meaning registered, several more.

"No it's not," Toni said calmly. "A revolution is when you can keep from getting trapped in your own metaphors."

"I don't know nothing about no metaphors," Makar said.

"I know you don't," Toni said. "Just don't try to pass that off as your long suit."

"You talking about long suits, but you ain't got no cards. You know what I mean? You ain't got no tricks. You talking about sex and song, junior, but you ain't said nothing about money. You know what I mean? You talking about long suits because your drain's frozen."

"Don't call me 'junior'," Toni said.

"Everybody sitting around here talking about where they going to live this winter. But ain't nobody talking about ditch weeds that I hear. You know what I mean? Everybody talking about beans and drawing pictures and Mr. Beethoven, but ain't nobody talking frozen drains. I tell you who's going to live here this winter. I done seen who's going to live here this winter. The cats going to live here this winter. You know the cats? Down there eating up the next day's food and messing the floor? I done seen em, they already here this winter, you know what I mean? Old car covered up with snow, what's-his-name there's van with all the flowers on it, and cats living in the upholstery. There's your cosmic dance, your utopia—cats know all about relax, because they know tension. I'll tell you about winter time. Winter time goes where the money is, and there ain't nobody talking about money. You talk about winter, you got to talk money or ditch weeds one, and ain't nobody here but me that knows ditch weeds, me and the cats. Ain't none of you going to get it from them. All you all know about cats is purring and messing the floor. You talking about weather, junior, but all you got is words. You come from South Carolina. That's where you from, ain't it, South Carolina? I know South Carolina. Words don't mean nothing in South Carolina. You think you know slave, but all you know is words."

"My name is Toni."

"What's that?"

"My name is *Toni*!"

"You're saying you think your name is Tony?"

"I *know* my name is Toni!"

"Tony what?"

"You don't have to act like a fool, you know."

"I thought Tony was a man's name. Is that the way you talk in South Carolina? Some of your best friends is slaves, you just don't know no names? Still think greed's got to do with money?"

She turned away in disgust.

"You ain't a man, are you?"

"How would you know?"

"I know what you're talking about. You're talking about you think you know your name is Tony. Tony who? I don't know no Tony. You talking about knowing what you mean, but you ain't talking about what you mean. You mean greed is what you mean. You're the slave. You don't know frozen drain because you don't know nothing else. The question is, Tony who? That's simple enough question—cept when you don't know the answer. Cept when you don't want to live there yourself. I gotcha Tony—you know what I mean?"

"You *think* you got your Toni! Kiss my ass!"

"Do which? You might think it's a kiss. You from Swishy Tail, down there where not even the cats know winter time, but you still know how to talk, is that what you saying? Words don't mean nothing in South Carolina, but Swishy Tail knows how to talk? Is that what kind of fool you was talking about acting? Relax into the tension? Un-huh. Un-huh. You don't want to live here yourself, you just want to relax into the tension? There's more than one Camp Farmington around here, you know what I mean? I mean don't come around talking about revolution unless you want to get trapped in your metaphor. That's what you said, ain't it? Don't want to live here yourself, you just want to relax into the tension? Just want to get trapped in your metaphor? You talking about waiting around for the answer, but you don't know what the question is, and you don't know you don't know. The question is, Tony who? Relax into that tension, then talk about everything being a lie. Greed's the only slave you know —that's why you ain't talking money.... "

With her back half-turned to him now, Toni stared out the window, ignoring Meriwether who tried, repeatedly, to catch her eye.

"...Revolution go around and around, all it ever point to is the center, don't know where it's at till it knows the center. But ain't nobody talking about the center, just running around in circles, whole lot of never-minds. The center don't run around, it just sits there. Thing about the center is, it knows never-minds. Get your metaphor trapped there sometimes, maybe you know something. Ain't no tension in the center, ain't nothing but the lion's roar. That's all. It knows greed. Run around in circles the closest you get to the lion's roar is a circus, you know what I mean? Ain't no lions in a circus, just a bunch of house cats crapping in their cage, a bunch of clowns. Is that what you mean, trapped in your metaphor, trying to pass a cage full of shit off to a bunch of clowns? You talking about permanent community, but you don't know neither one. And you're a long way from knowing. A long way from knowing you don't know. It's Camp Farmington all right. All you talking about is who's going to run it. Just more never-minds. No better idea than I been hearing, don't make no difference who runs it. And you a long way from knowing that."

Toni got up and walked out.

And Meriwether jumped up and followed.

When she caught up, at the edge of the road, she put her arm around her, and Toni flung it away without a word, without breaking stride. A few steps farther on she spun around. "Get away from me!"

Confused and frightened, Meriwether followed her as far as the graveyard, some distance behind, not even trying to catch up, and then watched her walk diagonally down the hill, her arms folded across her chest, the downslope lengthening her stride, making her footfall heavy in the dark. The meeting over now, people were returning to their rooms, voices out on the road. A light went on in Van Velder, then another, then "Brown Sugar," too loud for a moment, then turned down. Hugging herself against the cold, she watched as Toni stopped at the lighted entrance to the projection room and petted Nietzsche briefly before disappearing into the Barn with a slamming of the door.

When she turned to go back, there Bobo was coming off the road into the graveyard. He seemed not to have seen her yet. Her first impulse was to hide, which she resisted for a moment—then followed. She ducked down behind a tombstone and curled up with her forehead on her knees.

When he was gone, she slipped out of the graveyard and ran, low to

the ground, to the Wish Hole in the middle of the open field. She had
never done anything like that, not even as a child, but it called up
something familiar in her, this running and hiding in the night, and for
a moment she lost herself to it, diving into the hole as though her life
depended upon it.

And lay there, breathing hard, her face pressed against the cold dirt
—astonished by where she was and what she was doing.

It was as though she were now in love with Toni, had been from
those first days—intent on the one thing, being there with what the
other woman wanted or needed. Perhaps she *was* in love with her—
she did not presume any more to know the first thing about love.
Watching the projection room like a soldier from a fox hole, she
waited for the cottage to go down there and find out what was going
on.

Finally she knocked on the door, called the other woman's name,
tentatively.

"Toni?"

It was like a child's voice, outside the mother's door.

Toni told her what was going on, exactly.

"You're married to the man who's got control of this place!"

"He doesn't! He's bound by what the trustees say. You've got to
take him on his word about that. If it weren't for Nathan this place
would still be a school."

"You might, but I don't. I don't *have* to do anything!"

Meriwether tried to take her hand, but Toni pulled away.

"What's the *matter*?"

"I want you to get out of here, I want you to stay away from me."

"*Why?* I don't understand."

"You don't *understanding anything!* You've already *got* that infection. You're going to wake up some morning and find out that *all* your
lies have come true."

Meriwether was speechless.

"Just stay away from me!"

"*Please,* what have I *done?*"

"Nathan doesn't own this place, neither does the board of trustees.
They're caretakers, by their own description. You want to know
what's going on—I'll tell you, exactly. A whole lot of *shit,* that's
what's going on. A big *charade!* They tell us to come here because
we're the kind of people who belong here, and then tell us to leave
when it becomes obvious that *they're* not. School's over now—get in

your buses like good little kiddies and go home. And then they try to act like we're being obstreperous when we won't go. They want us to act like *we're* taking the place away from *them.*"

The bottom seemed to drop out of her with that—slowly, as her anger left her, she collapsed into a sitting position on the floor. Her glasses toppled off her head onto a mattress without a sound. As though something had hit her, hard, she didn't move. Arms hanging down, limply, between her splayed-out knees, she stared at the wall. A cat jumped up into her lap, then froze.

Without moving, Meriwether had collapsed right along with her, muscle for muscle, only the one life at work in the room now—the cat jumped into her lap too. All three of them were staring at the wall.

Toni looked up, near tears. "Maybe we can be friends later, but it's too confusing for me now. I don't want to have to think about you getting hurt." Her hands came slowly up between her knees, covering first her mouth, then her whole face. She was weeping.

Dropping to the mattress, Meriwether put her arms around her.

This time there was no resistance.

For a moment, as she felt Toni's arms slowly encircle her, Meriwether mistrusted her—it was the first time. Even then she didn't doubt the feeling between them, or suspect Toni of hiding anything, or of using her. She had no idea why she was mistrustful, or of what. The only sense she could make out of it was her own cowardice, her own heartlessness, her own self-protection. Toni frightened her—but it was no wonder. It was probably even for her own good.

Mason was crying up the hill.

"It's been a hard day," Toni said, wiping her face on Meriwether's sleeve. She tossed the cat from her lap. "Let's play some cards."

On their way up to Franklin in search of Rafe, Meriwether confessed that that remark about the infection had really gotten to her. She expected Toni to apologize, but she didn't—she in effect said the same thing again, in a friendly way.

It occurred to Meriwether—frightening thought!—that she meant it *literally.*

"Has Bobo got V.D. or something?"

"How would I know?" Toni said.

"Well how do you know I'm going to wake up some morning with an 'infection'?"

"I don't know."

To pursue the subject now seemed accusatory, but the more Meriwether thought about that answer the more puzzling it was. "You don't know *how* you know, or *whether* you know?"

Flapping her hands around her head and in front of her face as though beset by gnats, Toni laughed. And Meriwether dropped the subject, gladly.

On the bulletin board the next morning there appeared a card entitled HEISENBERG'S PRINCIPLES OF INDETERMINANCY, covered from margin to margin in Makar's best hand: SEX, LOVE, ANGER, HATE, PARENTAL CARING AND SHARING, CHILDISH REBELLION, FRIENDSHIP, COMPETITION, AGGRESSION, HOSTILITY, JOY AND HAPPINESS, CONFIDENCE, DEPRESSION, MADNESS AND SUICIDE, ANXIETY AND STRESS, CRIME AND PUNISHMENT, AGE AND LONELINESS, DEATH AND BEREAVEMENT, CONSCIENCE AND MORALITY, MAGIC, MYTH, SUPERSTITION, EXORCISM AND THE OCCULT, RELIGIOUS PASSION AND ECSTASY, HETEROSEXUALITY, BISEXUALITY, HOMOSEXUALITY, SADISM, MASOCHISM, FEMINISM, FETISHISM.

It was signed Ramon Mercader.

It was no ordinary crying, and Nathan was out of bed immediately.

The child was standing up in his crib across the room, in his blue crawler: gripping the bars and screaming.

"You're all right," Nathan said, lifting him quickly up and out. "You're all right!"

The child grabbed his neck and buried his wet face under Nathan's chin. Hot and sweaty all over, his small body was in spasm.

"You're okay, sweet child," Nathan kept saying, holding him tight and rocking him. "Daddy's right here."

When his eyes adjusted to the dark, Nathan saw what was going on: there was a cat in the crib.

Shifting the child to one side, he lunged for the animal with his free hand.

But it was out of the crib and gone.

The door was shut.

It was somewhere in the room.

It had to be.

"Daddy's right here," he kept saying.

He hugged the child tightly.

He swiveled his hips rhythmically, pressing the child's wet face against his neck.

He searched the room methodically with his eyes.

It was only then that he realized that Meriwether was not there. Her side of the bed was still made.

He went to the door, and listened, and then to the window, straining to hear. Listened for a radio somewhere, for sirens, for airplanes.

"Please, child! *Please!* Daddy's right here!"

Unable to leave the room to get his radio for fear the cat would escape, he returned to the search in desperation now. Instead of turning on the light he thrashed around the dark room with the child in his arms, kicking toys and clothes about, looking under the bed, and in the closet, pulling drawers out, throwing the curtains back, pulling furniture away from the walls. The child, who had begun to quiet down, became hysterical again, gripping his father's neck and screaming—but Nathan hardly noticed now. Realizing that all his flailing around was giving the animal even better places to hide, he became suddenly calm—which Mason recognized as no change at all. The child was screaming as his father pried him calmly loose and stuck him back in the crib, all the while comforting him by rote, and proceeded systematically to pile everything up in the center of the room. And then, when he was finished, to change his mind and systematically move it all into a corner. When it was finally established that there was only one place left that the cat could be, under the bed, he lighted a cigarette and analyzed the situation carefully. The child, exhausted now, was on his knees in the crib, still gripping the railing, his terrified face pressed between his upstretched blue arms, staring out wet and red through the bars. Nathan shoved the bed into the corner and barricaded a third side with drawers from the chest. Then with one hand he lifted the bed. And when the cat dashed out, he trapped it with his foot against the wall.

It was one of the cats from down the hill.

One of Toni's cats.

He wanted to strangle it. To bash its head against the wall.

Why not?

There was no reason why not.

As if to show that to the cat, he held it out at arm's length in both hands like a mirror, and banged its head slowly, deliberately against the wall, once—oblivious to the hind feet clawing his wrists.

And then, moving very quickly all of a sudden, he opened the door, gathered the whimpering child up in his free arm, and holding the cat out by the scruff of the neck went down the stairs two at a time.

He heard voices on the sunporch.

Shushed Mason, and listened.

Then stole through the dark kitchen with his hand over the child's mouth, into the library, and stopped where he could see without being seen.

Meriwether and Toni and Rafe were sitting down to a game of cards on the sunporch. An old floor lamp was pulled up next to the table, and Nietzsche was asleep on the straw rug.

Nathan kicked the glass door open and stood there shaking the cat at them like a fist.

"This goddamn animal was in Mason's crib! Keep it out of my bedroom or I'll kill every goddamn cat in sight!"

And with that threw it into the room and slammed the door.

Not until he was back upstairs did he have any idea what the child had been through.

Mason was streaked with blood.

"Everything is okay now," he kept telling him. "That's my blood, not your blood. The cat scratched *me*. Daddy is really sorry about that cat, *really sorry*."

He washed the blood off, tied a handkerchief around his wrist, straightened up the room, and took Mason into the big bed with him. Soon the child was asleep, and Nathan drifted into a fantasy in which they were alone together out in the snow with only a few walnuts for food. He rationed the nuts out to the child, saving the shells. Mason was a lot older, seven or eight, and when he asked why the shells were being kept Nathan told him that they could have some nutritional value. He found it impossible to deal with the child's death, even in a fantasy, so he imagined sacrificing himself as starvation approached so that Mason could survive—fascinated like a movie with images of preparing his son to feed on his body, that most excruciating of all educations, and with images of it actually taking place....

Nathan cringed.

And took the sleeping child back to the crib.

He got a drink and a cigarette, lay down on top of the sheet, the crotch of his pajamas open to the breeze, and soon he was thinking about Swishy Tail. He lay there watching his cock enlarge slowly, creep down his leg, bend back over his thigh, and then stand erect, throbbing, the head continuing slowly to swell. He imagined her sitting on the bed next to him watching it, staring at it. Makar was there too, watching them both. The bandages on his wrists trailed across his testicles like fingers. Everything that he imagined among the three of them was exciting, but Meriwether kept getting into it, and once she was in he was uncertain what to do with Makar. He tried at first to edit him out, but that was not what he wanted either. He couldn't find it.

When it was over he was ashamed.

And drifted off soon into another fantasy, one that he often had, in which he was in traction, paralyzed and impotent while Meriwether was still young. How he got there varied from version to version, sometimes sickness, other times a war or a domestic accident, lately he had thought it more likely that he had been shot in the spine while working undercover. But the burden of the situation was always the same: lying in bed at home all day every day, he watched Meriwether's life consumed in caring for the house, for their child, and for him— unable to offer her anything in return. He imagined that when he could not stand it any longer he persuaded her that she must go ahead and find another man, someone to sleep with at least. When she did, he imagined what it would be like to overhear the phone calls, to see her leave the house and return after several hours flushed with excitement, imagined what it would be like to meet the man, or not to meet him. When, in another version, she would not be persuaded, he imagined that his relief would be followed before long by an unbearable guilt. He always worked the fantasy through to a situation in which there was nothing left for him to do except kill himself, only to imagine that his paralysis was such that he could not do even that.

Several years ago he had confessed that fantasy to Meriwether, who at the time had her own troubles, a housewife and expectant mother whose husband was surrounded all day by art students, and her sympathy and understanding had proved invaluable. She saw it as the fantasy of a man who identified his ability to love and be loved with his cock, and a recognition of the paralysis of such an identification. That helped, it helped a lot, but what spoke most deeply to him was her insistence that under such circumstances she would find his concern for her sex life silly at best. She did not want another man, thank you, or need one. She convinced him that her feeling toward him would not change no matter what happened to him, paralysis, fame and fortune, even if he stopped loving her she would still love him.

"You mean..." he said.

"I love *you,* you crazy man," she said, "not your pretty cock, not what you *do* for me, can't you understand that?"

"I guess not. I'm always amazed. You always amaze me."

At such moments Nathan was like a child waking up from a nightmare in the arms of his mother.

When Meriwether came up to bed, he tried to explain what had happened with the cat, and to apologize. She was not nearly as hostile as he expected her to be; in fact, hard as it was for him to believe at first, she seemed not angry at all. She understood perfectly about the cat, said that she would have felt much the same way.

"You crazy man," she said. "I wish you could have seen yourself standing there in that doorway in your pajamas with Mason under your arm shaking that cat at us. You looked like something Munch thought up."

He untied the handkerchief and showed her his wrist.

"It looks like you tried to slash it."

"I guess I sort of did," he said.

He was so relieved he thought he was going to cry.

Everything seemed possible again.

They were close now, once more—crazy as it was. He did not understand the first thing about women. He did not understand the first thing about anything.

"I'll bet you want to make love," she said.

He did not—he was not even sure that he could. But he could not bring himself to explain why. "How did you know?"

"How could I not? I still can't. We've got some talking we've got to do."

He wanted to believe that somewhere in what she was saying, in what she was doing, she was telling him that she *did* want to, she always *wanted* to, it wasn't that. "Seriously—why don't you think about going back to Cambridge until you can get that thing cleared up?"

"You trying to get rid of me or something? Now that things are getting interesting?"

"What in the world was going on in that meeting tonight? I've never seen Makar..."

She interrupted him. "*You* started it, you know! I'll tell you one thing, I certainly didn't appreciate you sitting there letting him talk to her like that!"

It was hardly the first time since those early arguments that Toni had been mentioned, but it was the first time that there seemed to be something further to talk about. He welcomed the prospect, but he dreaded it too.

"You're really... getting something from her, aren't you?"

"Look, it's tearing me in half for the two of you to.... You don't have to like her, but...."

"You're really plugged in down there, aren't you?"

"She's a great person, Nathan. She really is. She's changing my life."

"Are you having an affair with her?"

They were sitting side by side, their pillows turned up on end, their backs against the head board. What she saw, with the light coming from behind him, was a wild gourd of hair: his small eyes furtive in a small mask of skin, surrounded by beard. He looked like a rodent peering out of a grassy hole. It occurred to her that that must be what Toni saw when she looked at him: his beady brown eyes in the midst of all that hair, his pink little mouth, toothless: when he talked it looked as though his beard were eating air, gumming it.

"Can't you think of anything but *sex*!"

He looked up at her as though she had slapped him.

She felt as though she had—only it wasn't her any more. It was Toni. She hadn't known she was that angry—she hardly knew it even now. To her it felt like Toni's anger.

"It's not what's going on *down there*—it's what's going on *right here!* You want to know why we haven't made love in six weeks? I'll tell you why, exactly. Because I haven't *wanted* to, that's why! That's the real reason. You think all I have to do is try. You don't understand I can't *do* it anymore, I *can't* try, it feels creepy! You don't know the first thing about Toni, and never will. She's *beyond* sex!"

"Can you give me some idea what I do wrong?"

It wasn't something that he did—it was him.

But how could you tell anybody that?

"You ask a bunch of creepy questions, that's what you do. It's not even sex you want, it's reassurance. It doesn't *work* that way. It *can't* work that way."

She knew what he was going to say—that he understood everything, that he thought she was right.

"I agree," he said. "You're perfectly right. We need to get away from here, that's what we need to do. We haven't had any *time* together in the past six weeks."

"It was that way *before* we got here, Nathan. I just didn't know it. I didn't know what to do about it. I still don't. *It's not the place."*

"Makar's right—it's one big vicious circle here. All due respect to Toni McHugh—I'll take your word for it. But I'm going to tell you something else about her. It's not just the projection room. I think it was unconscionable for them to come here to split up—and get *paid* for it. It would be hard to calculate the influence that's had on this community. On *us."*

The anger went out of her like air out of a balloon. In a short second or two she was limp. The idea that Toni's marriage had anything to do with theirs seemed preposterous. He would not face the facts, he could not do it. Their marriage seemed hopeless to her. They both seemed hopeless. All her lies *had* come true, already.

Toni seemed far away, beyond recall. Meriwether couldn't even remember herself.

She took her husband's hand in hers, stroking the back of it. He was probably the only one there who didn't know about her and Bobo. How could she blame him for wanting reassurance? Suddenly she was full of shame—and knew it, momentarily at least, for what it was: the truest feeling of the entire night.

She was tired, she said, they were both tired. She really did love him —did he understand that? She did not want to hurt him.

"I've missed you," he said, wrapping his big hand around the back of her neck and pulling her head down on his hairy chest, his voice changing. "Just an awful lot."

"Don't."

"Don't what?"

"Maybe again someday, but not now. Okay?"

"I was assuming that we couldn't."

Suddenly she was furious again. Hadn't she just told him that there was no infection? Hadn't she just told him that she had been lying all this time? "Come on!" she screamed at him, slinging a pillow into his hairy face.

They tried to look at one another—but could not.

The Toni in her said no, obviously she hadn't told him.

Nathan's film with Makar did not work out anything like he imagined. From the selection of the cast on it made little sense to him, and there were many times when he regretted the money and wished that he had never gotten involved. He was expecting a little symbolic drama or dance involving the community heavies, but the cast seemed picked at random, and what happened when they all got together was inane at best. Dutifully he put it on film, but he was so convinced that it was nonsense he did not even send the footage off to be processed.

The sound track, however, was something else. Unable to face out the situation with Makar, Nathan found himself in the absurd position of making a sound track for a film that he knew now would never exist. On top of twenty-four dollars worth of tapes—not just one but four, of the best quality of course—he got hit for a bottle of wine, an expensive one, and then lunch at the Dairy Bar on the way back from Northampton. It was threatening to turn into something worse than the film itself, so hopeless in fact that Nathan gave up the struggle—which in light of what happened made him regret the way he had approached the film. The critical moment came at lunch: he was waiting for Makar to order the highest priced thing on the menu when he saw what his preoccupation with money was doing to him—and he was ashamed. It wasn't just the money either: it was the time wasted: it was the frustration of not getting what he wanted from Makar: it was the irritation of being involved in something over which he had no control. He saw what all that was doing to him—there it was, laid out in the difference between him and the black man across the table, who was way back in himself, all that showed was a smile, enjoying himself thoroughly, as he usually did—and Nathan was ashamed even of his shame. It too, he realized, was just another way of holding on, holding back. By the time they left the Dairy Bar he was talking to himself in Makar's voice—ain't nobody on your back but you, get your heavy self off maybe you can fly.

The sound track was to be made on the broken piano in the painting Barn, but first Makar wanted to go to the Music Shed. It was a clear, bright day, in the mid-eighties, and they were alone. Rhonda was practicing the flute somewhere far off, down the hill; Jerry was playing the piano in the Hexagon, first a Beethoven sonata, several times, then Schoenberg; later on somebody was using a chain saw, not at Farmington, on the other side of the hill. Chagrined to find himself hesitant to drink after the black man, Nathan took the first swig and passed the wine bottle to Makar—who refused, asking him please to fetch glasses. When Nathan got back from Franklin with paper cups, Makar was stripped down to his pants and was into the corduroy bag of noisemakers. He went through all of them, banging and rattling and whistling perfunctorily as he had at the church, but then he went back through them again, this time with more purpose, as though he were circling something. Nathan got out his cameras, three of them, and loaded them and fitted them with different lenses, and when Makar noticed he asked him please to get wine glasses if there were to be pictures. And so Nathan left his cameras on top of the piano and returned to Franklin to exchange the paper cups for two long-stemmed wine glasses. Served him right, he thought—nigger-lip indeed! When he got back the black man was at the piano, playing with his eyes closed, and Nathan poured him a glass of wine and hurried the tape recorder into place. Makar got up, took the tambourine, and worked himself into a trance, a sweaty trance. With his eyes still closed he stripped off his pants, circled the piano like an animal, and sat down, moaning, at the keyboard. Quickly Nathan started the tape, picked up his cameras, and backed off. Makar was moaning, his head thrown back in a moan, a kind of gutteral cry, the veins standing out on his neck, his muscles were on him, and the sweat, and his feet were walking, not on the pedals but sideways: his naked feet were walking out from under the piano, as though something in him were leaving. Something in him leaving something else behind, bent over the piano, its face down on the keyboard at times, turned sideways, its ear close to the keys, its elbows higher than its shoulders. With a flip of his head he threw the leatherstrap toby over his shoulder onto his back, and then got down into the music with his whole body.

Soon he reached such a frenzy that he jumped up and started beating on the piano, first with his palms, then with the keyboard cover, slamming it down again and again. Soon that too reached an awful frenzy, and abandoning the keyboard altogether he leaped naked up on the cabinet, his testicles hanging down between his legs—and crawled in with the strings. Nathan, hiding behind his camera and his picture taking, kept it all framed neatly: he saw the black man going away and tried to follow, but for him it was all happening behind glass. The piece, named on the tape afterwards, was called "For A Brother in the Street." When it was finished Makar sat on the piano stool with his back straight and his eyes shut for a long time, resting, and then he came slowly back to the Music Shed, drank some wine, walked around. The sweat dried, changing the light on his skin. They did not talk. Nathan hung back with his cameras, sipping wine, uncertain what to do, doing nothing.

He kept thinking about that day with the gun at Diana's Pool, hearing that voice. It was teasing him—with things he couldn't remember even having heard. He knew no Spanish, didn't remember any Spanish being spoken that day, and yet out of nowhere the words of a song came to him in Spanish, *Para subir el cielo, se necessita un escalere grande, un otro chiquito*—which the voice then translated, *For climbing to the sky all you need is a tall ladder and a small one*—adding one acerbic comment, *good God!*

When Makar sat back down at the piano it soon became obvious that the first tape was just a warm up. A few minutes into the second and he was playing with his elbows and forearms and the backs of his hands, chants and moans and howls sectioning out of his wide red mouth like a loose-jointed dance in space: his body went free at the ties, into the music, pulsing. Light spun off him and around him as though sweat were its source, he shone, and right in the middle of it all his red mouth leaped about like a fire, scaring changes all over his face and body. Like an accelerating cone, brighter the music and faster, he went down with it, spinning, and kept going.

Circling the piano with his cameras, Nathan saw it happening and felt the suck where the black man went in, the pull, and saw him throwing his changes back up like wreckage in a whirlpool, a whole drama of figures coming and going in a whirl. What he perceived through his lens was not getting brighter and faster but was dimming and slowing down. The day was still bright and clear, not a cloud in the sky: his wife was playing with their child in the front yard of

Franklin, some two hundred yards away: the cook in the kitchen down the hill had not even begun the evening meal: Jerry was still practicing Beethoven in the Hexagon across the field, the sunlight on the score bouncing back onto his beautiful face. But for Nathan in the Music Shed with his cameras the light was turning down, everything was being sucked slowly but steadily down and in. At one point, working in the warped space of a 24mm lens, he saw it all come folding back the other way, like the wings of a mirror: he felt as though he were atop a ladder that suddenly had nothing to lean against. When Makar started the second tape, Nathan was shooting at 1/125 at f/8, but he shot only a few frames before the light seemed to fail and he doubled the exposure, and only a few frames there before he knew without ever taking the camera from his eye that even that wouldn't do and doubled it again, and then again, until soon he was shooting with the aperture wide open. He was not conscious of hearing the music, or even of seeing Makar as he played—just of the light, and of the shapes of things, and of the way they were disposed within the frame. Everything seemed to be in slow motion, he had all the time he needed, was anticipating rather than reacting, the shutter seemed to be releasing itself. For the first and the last time in his life he could have spit into a swinging jug. When 1/125 wide open seemed not enough, he cut the shutter speed, and cut it again, and again, doubling the light over and over on down until he was shooting one second hand-held exposures wide open, shooting them almost as fast as he could advance the film and get another camera and then as fast as he could reload. He photographed for over twenty minutes, letting more and more light onto the film.

When the second tape was done Makar took the microphone and named the piece "Theory of Transcendental Numbers for the Beloved Bird," dating and signing it. Then he slid off the piano bench and stretched out face down on the floor, his sweaty black body motionless.

And Nathan went outside and took his cameras off and lay down in the grass and folded his arms over his eyes and went immediately to sleep.

He thought at first he was dreaming, but then he realized that the man was back at the piano. He started to scramble for the tape recorder, it was extraordinary, this music, but something told him just to lie there and listen. It was as though there were another music in him, just as there was another voice: none of the frenzy of his own, none of the roughness, but formal, precise, subtle, a classical jazz full of allusions to other music. It began with a lyricism, a kind of elegant background music, perfectly conscious of itself for exactly what it was, pretty but not taken in by its prettiness, a kind of entertainment that offered suggestions of deepening. Which it did about a third of the way through, began easing down into an ever-tightening exchange between the two hands, the left working steady variations on the same bass chord, the right dancing high up on the keyboard—the two very slowly, deliberately converging. And Nathan began to hear a kind of story in the music, two parts of the same life interacting, the one heavy and deep and persistent, the other light, quick, elusive, charming: work and play perhaps, or character and personality, or man and woman, or body and soul, or—as the story deepened into the ambiguity of which was which—all those things simultaneously. The first third then seemed to have been about youth, an easy aimless romanticism leading into the rigorous clarities of the middle years and the ever-deepening, ever-tightening dance between one power and another—the story of a lifetime, then, this music. As the left hand got slowly louder and more insistent, encroaching like death on the right, the buried argument surfacing, the real struggle joined, the right answered with an ever-maturing resourcefulness that was, for the time being anyway, equal to the challenge—a dance now, as the story deepened, of the spheres as well, the earth and the sun, the solar system in the galaxy, the great powers answering to the greater. Finally the left hand overwhelmed the right, and like a star collapsing in on itself, kept spinning down louder and tighter, three bass notes over and over, and then two, and finally one, over and over and over, a deep powerful austerity, fading now, growing quieter. It seemed as though the story would end in death, your ear pressed to a black hole of no-sound—but it did not. That one deep note collapsed into silence and then came back out the other side, a tinkling of the right hand reborn high up, floating through space, taking shape again, or more now like the idea of a shape....

He thought he was getting up to thank Makar, but he was asleep again.

Late that night, using the broken piano in the Barn, they made the sound track for the film. There was only one light on in the enormous room, a flood lamp in the corner on a telescoping stand, turned up to the high ceiling. A bunch of wine bottles from a recent party were arranged in a cryptogram on the floor next to the piano, a balloon tied to the neck of each—the strings played upon by Makar's performance. Although the tape he made lasted only a little over eight minutes, they were there for nearly two hours, the whole time—remarkably enough for such a well-trafficked place—alone. Several times Makar used the keyboard, but most of the music was made inside the back end of the broken piano, not with his hands but with his walking stick, plucking and raking it across the strings, occasionally striking the console—with his walking stick and with a harmonica. Nathan, his cameras put aside, so tired that he was glad there was not enough light to photograph, was sitting on a wooden folding chair with his legs crossed and his hands in his pockets and his eyes closed, listening to Makar strike music from the wrecked piano. The harmonica took him completely by surprise—he had forgotten that the man even had one. There was a pause in the harsh sound of the stick raking across the strings and slapping the wood, a pause...then the sound of the harmonica... incredibly plaintive...like no other sound he had ever heard from this man, melodic, a halting melody, utterly plaintive, utterly simple. It brought together the two musics from earlier in the day: for all the raking and banging much of the dissonance had gone, the anger very much under control now: the balloons, like tall flowers vexed by the wind, merely touched each other, fitfully, red, blue, green, yellow. And then, coming through the opening of a short silence as though it had been waiting there in the wings the whole time: this plaintive harmonica, a simple melody, halting, broken, rough at the edges, the notes long and slow, so quiet and so slow, as though they barely had the energy to remember themselves into sounds. The balloons swayed then, when they did, almost in unison. It reached back to a simpler time, reached way back and came slowly, painfully forward, a beauty and sadness in its labor. When those first notes came from the harmonica, like survivors of some old catastrophe dragging themselves out into the light again, Nathan's heart leapt, and his whole body labored against tears. It was speaking directly to him, this music: saying that we are not only cut off from what we love but that our love itself is divided—that we are fallen, into forgetfulness, and can no longer even sleep. Twice more in the course of the piece the harmonica came back. The third time, toward the end, you were waiting for it. Nathan's whole body yearned for it, and when it came, so heavy now with hurt and loss, and yet not broken, his eyes filled with tears and he leaned forward, uncrossing his legs, and put his face in his hands. A long silence followed the end of the music. Nathan sat there on the folding chair with his face buried in his hands. The tape recorder was running, the only sound in the big hollow Barn. And then he heard Makar moving again, his bare feet on the wood floor. He picked up the microphone, cleared his throat, and said, "This is called, For Nathan." He paused, a long pause. "This is called, For Nathan. Farmington, Massachusetts, July 17, 1969." He paused again, then said, matter-of-factly, "So they say."

When they left the Barn, Makar took two of the wine bottles with the balloons, and as they parted he handed one to Nathan. And then, facing one another in the cool night under the stars, they smiled and embraced. Silently, on the same cue, they put their arms around one another and embraced. And went their separate ways.

As he was passing through the graveyard Nathan heard what he thought was an owl in the woods over on the next ridge, and he stopped to listen. It wasn't an owl—it was Makar whistling on the lip of his wine bottle. Nathan blew on his in reply. And after a moment he was answered back, this time at some distance, from up around Diana's Pool. Impossible—there was no way Makar could have moved that far that fast—then the first whistle came again from the same place. So there were three of them! Holding the balloon string away from the lip with his forefinger, Nathan whistled again, with a little flourish this time. And in answer a fourth came back, this one from down at Van Velder. And then a fifth, from up around the Music Shed—each distinct in its sound as well as its location. Makar was heard from again, several hundred yards on down the ridge. Only there was no certainty now who was who. Nathan was drawn out of the graveyard and up the hill toward Franklin—something told him where to stop and whistle again. For the next hour or so they walked all over Farmington, whoever and however many they were, whistling back and forth to one another like whippoorwills in the dark. It was as though they were mapping the place, in a language all its own. There was never any question in Nathan's mind—or perhaps it was his body —where to go next. They moved one another about like magnets, those strangely disembodied whistlings in the night. Slowly the intervals increased, and the song died out. And finally it was silent again all over Farmington. Nathan was in the Wish Hole, sitting with his legs crossed and his eyes closed, the bottle still in his hands. The whole place lay around him now in a way it never had before, the fields, the hills, the ridges, the buildings, the people, a new idea of the place surrounded him, embodied in the silence. This was the Farmington he had been trying all along to envision. Without opening his eyes he pulled the balloon string loose from the bottle and let it go. And when he looked up he saw several other balloons drifting up into the starry sky, shapes now not colors, and as he watched, several more, trailing their strings in a kind of dance.

The photographs he made that day in the Music Shed were unlike anything he had ever done. The images were saturated with light: a blurred grey figure floated in a white space, the light eating away at the shape, arms and legs gone in some to a crooked line, a foot eaten away by light to a black needle: recognizably human, even recognizably Makar at times, but unearthly, more presence than person. He printed and mounted two full sets, and with great pride presented one to Makar—who looked at them carefully but matter-of-factly. On the second time through he singled out one image in which the light had nearly eaten away the figure and said that that was where he lived a lot of the time. And then he handed the stack of prints back with the only other comment he made, delivered it seemed to Nathan in all innocence.

"That's some camera you got," he said.

"They're for you," Nathan said, trying to give the prints back. "They're a gift."

"Naw, they ain't."

Nathan was disappointed and irritated, accusing Makar privately of not understanding any art but his own. In time, however, he came to see that Makar's response was far more clear-headed than his own—what kind of camera indeed! And to think, vainly, that he understood what the man meant when he said that the pictures were not a gift.

On the night of the first moon landing, Nathan, who was carrying the only TV set at Farmington up the hill in the dark, came across Makar poking around in the Wish Hole with a walking stick.

"Hey!" he said. "You scared me!"

Makar chuckled.

Nathan waited for him to say something. Squatting in the enormous crater—the 'stage' for a play by Rafe that had no script other than the preparation of the hole itself, at the geographic center of the community—Makar stared up at him, holding the stick between his legs with both hands, and said nothing.

"What's the word?" Nathan asked him, a smile in his voice.

"Pieta," he said.

"Oh yeah?"

"It loves to happen."

There was a pause. Nathan waited. Makar chuckled.

"You mean the moon?"

"That's one of em," he said.

Nathan wanted to stop, sit down, talk.

Why not?

Using the TV for a stool, he arranged a place as close as possible, his feet on the lip of the crater.

"How many are there?" he asked.

"It loves to happen," Makar said again, and chuckled, out of the back corner of his mouth.

"There are probably four or five things that love to happen," Nathan said.

"Not four or five," Makar said.

"Three?"

"Seven."

"I got you!"

"It's called An Alternative Education Experience," Makar said.

Nathan laughed.

"You know what I mean?"

"I think so."

"Alternative. All Turn Native. Alter Native."

Nathan laughed again.

"Un-huh," Makar said.

"So that's the word — seven?"

"Pieta. It loves to happen."

"I can believe that."

"Where you think you going?"

"To watch the landing."

"Un-huh. That's where you think you're going?"

"You know different?"

"That's what they tell me."

"It loves to happen!" Nathan said.

"You got it," Makar said. "But I wouldn't pay a whole lot of attention to what people say."

"How's that?"

"People get in-tell-i-gent, they don't want to get eat up by the moon."

"Is that what's happening up there?"

"I don't know nothing about no 'up there'," Makar said.

"The landing."

"I don't know nothing about no 'landing'."

"Mum's the word then?"

"It's one of em," Makar said.

"Why did you come to Farmington?"

"Same reason you put the ad in the magazine, I reckon."

"Food and money? Lots of attention?"

"Reasons your business, not mine."

"Everybody needs food and money."

"Indeed they do."

"And everybody wants attention."

"That's you talking."

"Then why did you come?"

"Food and money's fine with me."

"I don't believe you. I think there's more to it. Did you come here to teach?"

"Anybody go someplace to teach ain't likely to have much worth learning when he gets there. Nobody goes no place anyway, they gets taken."

"You mean the whole World Teacher thing came from us?"

"Ain't no other place for it to come from, is there?"

"If we're missing the point, can't you make it some other way?"

"If I was making points I reckon I could."

"That's just me talking—you've had your say?"

"Ain't nothing here but you, me and ditchweeds. Not that I can see."

"Why did you beat up Bobo?"

"He wanted beating, I reckon, and I wanted doing it. We was just passing headaches I guess you'd say."

"You're not trying to justify what you did?"

"Justifications your business."

"Do you think you're beyond good and evil?"

Makar chuckled. "Beyond good and evil ain't nothing but good and evil moved on down the road."

"You mean you came to Farmington because the ad you saw appeared on page one hundred and three?"

"Ninety six."

Nathan laughed. "Do you mean that literally or figuratively?"

"Listen to him! Least you asking real questions now. I'm going to tell you something—you ready? Ain't no such thing as a figure. Because there ain't nothing else. Closest thing either one of us ever saw to a literal is what's-her-name, and look at her. Or you."

They were both smiling now, at each other.

"Will we ever see you again? When the summer's over?"

"I don't know nothing about no *again*."

"We haven't seen you for the first time?"

"When you ready, you'll see. It won't be me, not what you're talking about."

"It'll be ourselves we're seeing?"

"That's what it'll look like for a while, more'n likely. But there ain't nothing to that either, not what you're thinking. Let me ask *you* a question. You ready?"

"Is that the question?"

'Listen to him. Might as well be. Un-huh, un-huh, might as well be. You ain't crazy, you just act like it."

"I'm ready."

"For what?"

"Whatever."

"What's that?"

"I don't know. You haven't asked me the question yet."

"Why'd *you* come here?"

"I don't know."

"Naw. You're a long way yet from not knowing."

"Because I'm on my way to watch the moon landing?"

"You asking me?"

"Okay, I got it!" Nathan said, standing up. "Thanks! See you!" He picked up the TV.

"You might just do it," Makar said.

o o o

When he turned on his side toward the window, gazing into the shadows across the room, he became conscious, on the periphery of his vision, of a light in the sky. It was much brighter than a star, and bigger, and it seemed to be moving at a fairly rapid speed across the sky near the horizon. But there was something about it that argued with those perceptions, told him that he didn't know where that light was, or what it was doing. When he looked directly at it he decided that it must indeed be out there in the sky—where else could it be? and that he was seeing it through the trees, though he could not figure out how, at such speed, through dense foliage, it remained visible for so long. He assumed that it was an airplane, and that, to appear to be moving so fast, it was close and at a low altitude. He listened intently. And when he was sure that he was not hearing anything, he became alarmed. Several people were still downstairs watching TV—if anything had gone wrong with the world surely he would be alerted. He kept waiting for the light to disappear, at least briefly, no opening in the foliage could be all that large, or disappear for good out of the window frame, but it did not. Inexplicably it remained, as bright as when he first saw it, brighter even. It seemed to be getting brighter and brighter. Perhaps it was coming toward him, but as best he could determine it seemed to be moving laterally, and at a great speed too—

though it seemed obvious now, all that notwithstanding, that it was staying this whole time in the same place. The harder he tried to confirm his perceptions the more disoriented he became. It was making him nauseated. A dog was barking somewhere, and he thought momentarily that would stabilize him, but it did not, it only added to the welling nausea. He shut his eyes in an effort to hold on to himself.

With the exception of Toni everyone in the community had been there, talking celebration, acting celebration—but celebration was not what it was. Right from the start the room was full of static and restlessness, something scratchy beneath the surface, crossways, and before long everyone was infected with it. When they talked they talked too loud, and when they listened they did not hear, and when they heard they quarreled or grew bored or became distracted, and there was a falseness in all the laughter and the merriment. The room was far too crowded. There was a popcorn fight that irritated even those involved. For the first couple of hours the trouble was all so vague, and what would pass for causes so trivial, that no one could get hold of any of it. But after a while a broad conflict shaped up and served for a time anyway to bring the tensions into focus. Those who thought that this was one of mankind's great moments—Nathan and Medders and David and Ellie and others—resented the irreverence of much of what was going on, and their resentment built toward a moment midway in the evening when Medders told Bobo and Rafe and by implication several others to shut up all their adolescent crap or leave. And that in turn was resented by many, some of whom became more irreverent, which increased the resentment all around—until finally they were into another of their catch-all arguments about the right way to live.

Toward the middle of the evening Makar appeared and took a seat in the library, just off the sunporch. From where he was sitting he could not see the TV, but you could not watch the TV without seeing him. He sat in a rocking chair holding his hands up in front of his face as though they had an independent life and watched intently as the fingers went through a whole series of formal exercises. There on the TV Walter Cronkite was following man's first documented landing on the moon, and there behind the set was Makar, mocking the whole idea. By the time Neil Armstrong put his left foot down on the lunar surface late that night, Makar was in the Wish Hole with his back to the moon, but he stayed long enough for a lot of people to get down on him. Some ridiculed him for thinking that he could compete with the space program; others, like Nathan, were embarrassed that he felt the need to. But they all ended up, despite themselves, watching his fingers as intently as he did.

No matter though who or what was blamed, no one could get a handle on what was wrong, and eventually the evening spun mean and wild. Rhonda, drunk, tried to seduce Medders, who was interested only in the moon landing, and Jerry got so upset that he had to leave and go to his room; whereupon Rhonda threw a cup of hot tea on Medders, and Meriwether, upset to begin with because Toni was not there, took to screaming, first at her, then at others. By then Bobo and Rafe were smoking openly, right in front of Nathan, passing joints to anyone who wanted them, and Nathan left and came back and left again. By the time he decided to deal with them they were gone, and he chewed out the first woman who opened her mouth, Holly, who was having a fight with Keith because he was flirting with Rhonda. She left in tears, which set Meriwether off again, accusing Nathan of trying to dominate the evening. One insult and bitchery and brutality followed another, pettiness, confusion, chain smoking, the slamming of doors. Finally Nathan, who had been looking forward to Apollo 11 all summer, could not take it any longer and went to bed.

He shut his eyes, trying to disconnect himself from that light, but whatever it was had a hold of him now. It was under his skin: it was coming in spasms around his eyes: his whole face was twitching: he felt little things driving themselves against his eyeballs, first from underneath, them from behind. One minute he felt as though his head was being invaded, wave after wave of tiny things coming from one direction and then another, the next as though muscles he hadn't known were there were going into spasm. For all that was upsetting about it, however, it was not altogether unpleasant now. He was also fascinated by what was going on. It was as though he was being possessed—by his own body. He kept his eyes shut until that too began to nauseate him. When he opened them the light was still there, brighter than he remembered, and moving faster. And that dog was still barking. He had lost all sense of time, but there was no question now that if it were an airplane or even a UFO it would have disappeared long ago. When he tried to look directly at the light it seemed to jump wildly about, and to threaten to grow so bright as to blind him. Fear of it began to overwhelm him again. The only way he could keep from getting sick was to look at something else. The light then seemed to stabilize on the periphery of his vision, and he could understand it as an uncommonly bright star, given illusions by the wind-blown trees. That was where it kept him for a long time, watching it out of the corner of his eye. When he was awakened by Meriwether later, bringing him a fried banana in a tea cup, he could not believe that he had been asleep. The light was gone, but the dog was still barking.

Nietzsche was with her, all around her, barking, leaping into the air, darting in to nip at her flying feet—down the hill they ran in the darkness and through the graveyard and around the Barn and out into the field again, her cape flying. She had what she had gone after, Warren's pipe, and she carried it like a torch, in parody, and she was looking now for the big pile of dirt on the other side of which, in the Wish Hole, waited Rafe and Makar, sitting just as she had left them she assumed, their arms wrapped around their knees. There it was, there indeed it was, and like everything else she came on this evening, or that came on her, there was a surprise in its sudden appearance, a kind of magic, new footing to contend with, new meanings to accommodate; it was the brilliance of her performance tonight that it found its occasions in such surprises, that it took all obstacles and advanced her inclinations on them, transformed the potential fall into the next nuance or acrobat of body, magic to magic, what was in the way became the way in—and so she ran headlong the weight of the hill-slope and her tiring body behind her up the dirt piled high on the lip of the hole, her momentum playing out at the top, Nietzsche right with her in a barking slip-legged struggle to keep loose dirt under foot. And she paused there, on the fulcrum of her act, several feet above the two men sitting like Mexicans in the hole, drawing the cape around her like an old movie at the roof's edge. And then, in a move too graceful and intense to be simply parodic, pirouetted histrionically and fell in a dying swoon down the loose dirt embankment into the hole—rolled over and over and over, the cape tightening into a cone, spinning off dirt as she rolled, the dog barking wildly. And came to rest on her back between the two men with her eyes closed and a smile all over her face, breathing hard, her chest heaving. She giggled. Nietzsche was barking and licking her face and neck. She held the pipe out for someone to take, her eyes still shut.

They sat cross-legged in a circle and smoked. First Rafe, then Makar, then her, then around again, in silence. Slowly the charge built, by thirds, flaring at arm's length in the pipe bowl, turning them around and down. Each time the pipe was passed it got harder to handle, eye to eye, they were in the tunnel now, under some pressure, inhaling it deeply, the spiraling pitch of sirens going both ways at once, rifling them down to some small explosion at the end. For they all knew now that they were smoking together in order to blow Rafe out of the hole. And so instead of handing the pipe at arms length they rolled on their hips and came face to face, knuckle to knuckle, checking out who knew what. His visage of thick lips put a move on her, a mirror, a tease, black, and then gone, leaving her with the pipe in her hand—you could never tell what that face was doing, that smile. She realized then what she had felt a moment ago with the side of her knee: the gun strapped under his arm. The next time he came around he had never been so close, his eyes hanging in front of hers—she flinched. Without a word Rafe was expelled. And without a word, without looking back, he left, climbing out of the hole and disappearing across the field into the darkness. Leaving her and the dog alone with Makar, the lid off. The call of an owl in the woods, tall, alone, lifted the world up in the moonlight and leaned it toward her. She was afraid. And saw, in the quick spins of her mind, her own frightened face beaming: the light coming from within: her fear in profile gone to light. There he sat looking at her. They were out of control now, or getting there— what was she afraid of, she thought, except that they could do no wrong.

She was smiling. She was lying on her back, and the dog was standing next to her, and she was rubbing his belly, stroking his powerful furry chest sloping to the hairless stomach, back and forth. He was motionless now, the dog, having positioned himself for the most pleasure, his tongue out, panting, his eyes half closed and dreamy, his innards sucked up like a yogi to purify sensation. She trailed the palm of her stroke farther back each time, whispering to his sex.

Makar was standing over her now, looking down. A large dark triangular shape moved upward like a pyramid and folded over him like a cape and his eyes were in it, hanging there, as though they were cut out of the dark. He was gathering slowly forward, toward the crown, toppling slowly into her space as though she were sucking him in. And then he was folding back the other way, as though he were sucking her slowly up. She quivered and shut her eyes and shook him off. When she opened them again the tent was gone and he was standing there in his shape, his eyes staring down at her. A sky full of stars behind him. The moon floating high off his shoulder like a balloon. Thumb to thumb, finger tips to finger tips, she put a frame around him, bobbing it up and down as though he were pulling the string, as though the comic moon were his thought. And her thought was...for a change she didn't have one. In the next frame she lifted her knees and spread them, let them fall away to the sides, breathing at him like gills. And then she unbuckled her levis and worked them down, her panties, and brought her knees together and pushed them down and off, kicking them away, and then let her knees fall open again and the fingers of her left hand begin slowly to part the hair between her legs—a slow two-step of fingers, feeling their way into the part, sorting, combing, the first and little fingers spreading the labia, carefully, her eyes on his, the barest trace of face around his large eyes—then with the other hand she touched herself. With the forefinger of her right hand she found the open circle of her clitoris, pinning it gently to her pelvis, massaging it in a circle on top of that hard mound of bone.

He was standing there watching her masturbate, all the time staring at him. He put his foot between her legs, his big toe over her forefinger, riding it around, pressing gently, then underneath it, the sole of his toe gently on her, around and around. She held his big toe between her thumb and forefinger, guiding it, playing with the pressure, watching his cock swell under his pants along his thigh. She touched it with her foot, running her toes slowly up and down the shaft.

"Un-huh. Un-huh," he said.

He took it out and showed it to her. He shook it at her. With his thumb and index finger ringed tight around the base he shook his hard cock at her like a blackjack. He was telling her, she realized, that she had no idea what was going to happen next. His face was liquifying in that smile, she was liquifying.

She swooned, she shut her eyes and writhed and swooned, quickening the pace on herself, both hands now, her hips bouncing in quick short strokes on the ground, faster, and then she pitched up in the hips and smoothed out in a long ohhh and her head fell over on her shoulder, ohhhh, and then her head was thrown back, pitching from side to side, her neck white in the moonlight, a look of anguished pleasure on her face, and then she collapsed, quivering, and rolled from side to side, her thighs squeezed tight now, clutching her hands between her legs and moaning.

Then she was quiet, looking up at him, beginning to smile again.

"What can I say?" he said.

It was not his voice.

She wheeled around, to one side, then the other—as though she were just as frightened as she had been the first time she had heard it, that night she and Rafe had been held prisoner—then all the way around, giggling.

No one else was there.

Just the two of them—the third this time was Nietzsche.

"The quality of affection is everything, as I'm sure you know. I feel like a fool even saying it. Obviously you have a better understanding of such things than I do, much better. At moments like this, among those who matter, there is much that is better left unsaid. I'm flattered, of course."

In one quick motion, as though he were throwing someone over his back, he slipped out of his dashiki and tossed it to the ground next to her levis. The gun was there, strapped under his arm. He slipped out of the holster, removed the weapon, tossed the holster after his shirt, and knelt down in front of her, resting his forearms on her raised knees— the gun, limp-wristed, against the inside of her thigh.

Her arms were wrapped around her chest now, her fingers gripping her shoulders, and she was staring at him, warily, the smile gone—just as she had that night in his room. She was answering his impersonation with one of her own—of herself.

"The occasion calls for wine, does it not? Wine and hawkbells?"

She stared, saying nothing.

"Does it not?"

Finally she nodded, once—what's-her-name to what's-his-name.

"You are perfectly right of course to be frightened. There is nothing any more dangerous in the world than a weak man with a gun, absolutely nothing. But it's merely for the dog to get used to. I have the deepest respect for animals. If there is one thing I wish I knew half so well as this handsome beast here, it is the absolute necessity of sniffing things out before you lie down. And of raising one's hind leg to as many things as possible—leaving such records of ourselves as we can. I trust you know that you have intimidated me. Such passion I am not used to. Watching you fuck yourself like that, one is left with a sense of

...I believe *inadequacy* is the vulgar language for it. Frankly I have never conceived of such passion, not in a pig's ass. Surely you don't still believe that you are interested in politics."

He stopped for a while.

He stared at her, smiling.

She knew that he didn't think that his white man was as sexy as he thought he was—but that was all she knew. He wasn't merely hiding. Nor was he merely jacking her around. He seemed to be calling for something in her, bringing something forth. At first she thought she was hanging back, her eyebrows raised questioningly—then she realized that that was it. He wanted her to play with him. She could feel it happening in her eyes, her mouth, in the way she held her head, at once coy and direct. Meriwether was the kind of woman the white man was talking to, a little wide-eyed all the time with wonder, a little frightened but not too.... It was no longer herself she was impersonating, she realized, it was Meriwether: the way she held her eyes, wide, from afar, unable at times even to look at you, an almost convincing display of innocence, almost exciting.... The kind of woman who talked about sex always as making love, who was terrified of V.D., who could lie without having to know it, or know it without having to understand it. She could feel it happening in the way she lifted her brows, and kept them there, her questioning charged with sincerity, her eyes at once wide open and sealed shut, always withholding. The kind of woman who played with her sex the way she played with her money—one minute wanting you to take it away, the next not. It was exciting, not knowing what was to happen next. Makar, it seemed, knew her kind well.

He dropped back into himself, snapping his fingers in front of her face. "Un-huh. Un-huh. I told you, didn't I? Ain't nobody here but you and me and nigger Joe. I'd be uncomfortable being anybody else, you know what I mean? I mean I'm going to eat your white asshole like a dog, and your white pussy. You know slave, you just don't know you know."

"Who *are* you?" The kind of woman who would ask that question as though she expected an answer, would not continue until she got one....

He answered with the white man's laugh, tossing the gun onto his shirt. He arranged himself so that he was sitting cross-legged between her open legs. He lifted her buttocks in his hands, and without taking his eyes off her ran his curled tongue very slowly up between her legs.

For a moment, as he was lifting her and getting down, she tensed up and withheld.... But when his tongue found her she gave way with a little spasm and a cry and reached out with her hands for his head....

"For the poor and for the black dignity is upheld by pissing in the streets. The rest, as the poet says, is art. Who am I indeed!"

His tongue, this time, was more playful. He knew the kind better even than she did, a little slavish but not too. She slipped deeper toward him, reaching again for his head, but again he was not there.

"In a state of exhaustion, civilization turns more and more to language. What your wise dog does with his nose, I do with my poor mind and my words—a troop of night-time children, dirty, singing in the streets of San Juan. *Para subir el cielo, se necessite un escalere grande, un otro chiquito.* And then imagine, come morning, a decapitated dog floating in the bay. In the exhausted morning light, floating among the common filth in Bahia de San Juan, the decapitated body of a big black dog. It loves to happen. We call it the Wish Hole, as if we knew where we were. And imagine that dog's head continuing in the belly of a shark. In one way or another we have been talking all summer about eating—wouldn't you agree? We have called freedom by many names, as if we knew something about it. But comes the clincher, the words get real. Imagine the smile on the dog's face. Perhaps it's an illusion, the final irony of decomposition—but then perhaps not. It could be the final impotence of all teeth laid bare, the only true smile—more nearly the decomposition of irony. That would be the day, would it not? Dogs run free, why can't we? The answer should be obvious enough. Once you see that dog's head awash in the guts of its exit you are in a position to observe that the eyes are the first thing to go, or perhaps the last—the pupils fade, the irises, the eyes turn all white, bobbing in the juice, they begin to lose their shape. Imagine that they are seeing more deeply, that the smile itself is the last thing they say. A smile without power, none, without intent. It's hard to imagine, isn't it? We talk of freedom as though it were yet something else to acquire, to strive for. Is it not possible that bondage is bondage, that language itself is a form of confusion? That each thing is already complete, whatever and wherever, always? That even Nathan himself is free, just as we know him? That even you are, railing at your captors? Captain Armstrong, dressed by a haberdasher from Kansas City, can hear the children singing in the streets, for after all they sing the same song, the first order of business an American flag, the next a golf club. But he can hardly imagine the dog, much less the dog's head smiling in the belly of a shark—hence his trip to the moon is on T.V. At this very minute he is adjusting the cameras for all the world to see, he is swinging his club, he is waving our flag.... You would have to say that it loves to happen...."

She had lost all general impression of him. There was the voice, the shape of his head between her legs, the feel of his hair now and again on the inside of her thigh, his ear in her hand and gone, the rough skin of his chin across her palm, his cheeks. There was the smell of him, and on the margins of it traces of his small dark room—the smell of being inside things, things that were inside things. And there was the voice, working her—she felt sometimes as though she were inside it—no longer had a general impression of anything—only his eyes staring up at her from the middle of it all, his teeth. She could see the nicotine stains turning down dark in the crevices between his teeth, the brownish tartar scalloped at the edge of his gums, his thick black lips, the bright red undersides, wet, the broad flat nose, the pores of his skin. In the hollows of his cheeks there were pores within the pores. She saw the tiny blood vessels in the whites of his eyes, exploding from the dark brown irises, and right in the middle the black pupils, rifling down. When she looked at the pupils, she lost sight of even the eyes. He frightened her. She wanted his cock in her hands, his balls.

He went back down on her, staying a little longer this time. She withheld at first, protesting, but he brought her around again, and up a little, curling the hard tip of his tongue inside her clitoris like an ampersand. She tried to lock his head in with her knees, his kinky hair, his scratchy face, but he pulled loose. This time she was angry.

So that was what happened next.

He wanted her to play rough.

"Perhaps I have gone too far too fast—the tone a bit too austere for the occasion? You can't relax without your tension? No fun, no sabe? I would be the last to disagree, most certainly under the circumstance. For what are we, after all, if not under the circumstance. Let's say then that the dog smiles no less cunningly at his new master. It's the same story, engaged in somewhat different terms—more dramatic, surely, and perhaps a little closer to the point. Once you have imagined the smile you have imagined both its cunning and its new master. Is that not correct? That is what I mean by the quality of affection, that is what you and I share—a certain fascination with dogs. With whatever runs free, as the song man says. Or have I misjudged you, misunderstood everything? Perhaps you still have other uses for me? Have come for my gun? Are still plotting a take-over? Have found the money?"

And then in Makar's voice, "Un-huh. Un-huh. You know what I mean? You know take-over, don't you?"

And then in her voice, appropriating her Meriwether perfectly, "Who *are* you?"

He chuckled. "That's the question all right, come three hundred sixty de-grees."

And she answered him in the white man's voice, with only the barest trace of tentativeness, "The new master. Is that not correct?"

He chuckled, and went back down, and this time he gave promise of staying. She kicked him in the side, hard, with her heel, in the kidney — promise of her anger if he didn't. They worked out the last awkwardness of their posture, until they were holding one another by the elbows. He went in with his curled tongue, in and up, slowly, and then in her with his rough chin, their eyes locked on one another now: he moved her in a tight wet circle with his chin: and she began to quiver — the way Meriwether was always promising to quiver, trying to let go. Just as she dropped her head back and shut her eyes, he broke off again.

"One last thing, and then I promise that I will never say another word for as long as I live. You must try to imagine the disgust that I feel when I look between another human being's legs and find nothing there, nothing. No cock, no balls. Your cunt, laid open as it is now in the moonlight before my eyes, looks exactly like this —

He stopped talking: was riding ever so slowly up on his knees, his face coming closer and closer, a big grin. It floated up through the frame of her legs and sailed calmly toward her. And then all of a sudden without a sound his fat lips curled back like an ape's and quivered, his whole face decomposed — a big red wound of soft quivering wet skin.

She screamed, scrambled back, kicking at him.

He was standing at attention on his knees, his arms at his side, his eyes shut.

She kicked him hard with her heel, in the chest, several times, and then in the face.

He was grinning.

She kicked him again in the face, hard—bringing blood to his mouth.

He lashed out, back-handing her across the cheek. Her head spun, her hair flew out like a skirt.

Suddenly they both stopped, eyeing one another tentatively.

She was making a strange sound, a giggly whimper.

"Un-huh, un-huh. Your pussy ain't up in your head at all, it's down in your feet. It loves to happen. The question is, Toni who—that's what I want to know. I'm going to show you your slave."

"I got your Toni," she said.

"Un-huh. Un-huh. You might just do it. I mean you got the club and the flag, but where you living? I don't know no Toni yet—just more never-minds."

She undid his belt, letting the heavy buckle turn over of its own weight into her hand. Slowly then she pulled the leather strap from around his hips a section at a time, pausing after each loop, her left hand pressed flat against his hard stomach—as though she were pulling the fuse out of a bomb, a slow step at a time, the excitement building—and then the last, the tongue snaking out on the ground between them. She laughed, almost cocky now. "I'll show you what loves to happen," she told him. She doubled the belt, dangling it in front of his face, showing it to him, tapping him on the nose with it, stropping his jaws, his chin, trailing it back and forth across his mouth—then withholding it. "Is this what you said you didn't see between my legs?" She hid it behind her back. "Was that it?" He said nothing. "Answer me!" She slapped him across the face with it, loud. Then back the other way. "You think you know slave? I'm going to show you slave!"

"You might just do it—once you get done adjusting the cameras."

She let the belt out and stepped back. "At least your own blood is real? Is that what you mean?"

He was still on his knees, his arms at his sides—that look on his face. Go ahead, he was saying—since you think you know what you're doing.

On the shoulder she slapped him, almost gently, half a belt. Then again, a little harder, on the neck. "You know slave all right, it's in your blood? Where *you* living?" She held the bloody belt in front of his eyes, his mouth, his nose, showing him—things weren't so cryptic after all, were they? He thought because he knew ignorance he was above arrogance, but arrogance was what she saw in his smiling face, not Birmingham, not Watts. He had it coming—she wanted to break him. "This one's for Bobo!" she said, unleashing the full belt around his shoulders, across his back. Smell it, Makar, taste it! "This one's for Jerry!" She was angry now, almost crying. "This one's for me!" With all her might she tried to swing—the look on his face stopped her.

Standing there in front of her on his knees, he was absolutely still. His face, streaked with blood, was a mask: only the eyes looked out: and in the middle of his eyes his pupils stood perfectly still, fixed on her. It was as though she hadn't even touched him yet. That's what he was smiling at.

He was smiling at her.

She felt weightless, as though she were falling through, slowly. They were like...they weren't like anything.... They were merely his eyes, without gravity, watching her. Nothing stuck to them, not even his own blood.

With both hands she broke loose, unleashing the belt—and he snatched it away from her, spinning her like a top. Jumping to his feet, he caught her, gently—as though suddenly they were dancing. He wrapped his arms around her, wiping his blood all over her body. He wiped his blood on her breasts, her stomach, her buttocks, her thighs —playfully, tenderly. "I'll show you what's in my blood," he said. With his hand he wiped it between her legs, gently. "Same thing that's in your blood." His wet fingers found her. "You know what I mean?" He lifted her off the ground as though she were weightless. She was sitting on a cone of his fingers. Her eyes were wide. She was smiling. They were both smiling.

"Wanna fuck?" she asked him.

"Might as well," he said. "Done got this far."

"Do you really believe that?!"

He was angry. She had never seen him angry at that particular juncture before—something in her found it exciting.

Both of them, she feared, were deeply pitiable now.

"Don't," she said. "Please don't."

"What do you expect me to do when you say that? Disappear? You're saying *don't* to who I am!"

"It's getting impossible," she said.

"Not unless you think it is."

Neither of them said anything for a while. Nietzsche was barking again down the hill—which meant that Toni was still outside, probably in their place, probably with someone else.

"We can work it out," Nathan said. "If we are willing to."

Work it out—she could scream.

"What do you want? Do you want to make love?"

"I did a while ago—and so did you."

Did a while ago—but doesn't now.

He probably believed that.

"Well then let's make love."

His eyes narrowed, and he stared at her.

She couldn't believe that he would come back around, with the feeling what it was between them—but she knew that he would.

She no longer felt trapped.

She felt nothing.

"Are you kidding?" he asked.

"If you want to make love, let's make love."

"Do you want to?"

"I might," she said, trying to smile. She felt exhausted. "You never can tell about me."

The next thing she knew he was on top of her, his beard was in her face, his heaviness.

"Are you still sore?"

"A little," she said, unable to look at him.

She believed that she was betraying Toni.

"Do you want to stop?"

"Just go slow."

"Tell me if it hurts."

She told him, and she told him. Everything in her except words told him that he was hurting her, that she did not want to be there, that she hated him and hated what they were doing—but he just kept doing it to her, his hairy face.

After a while it didn't hurt so bad—something else was calling for attention—and she began to move with him. It was down there some-where, laboring to be known, some turn of memory, a position, a lust, a fantasy, some anything that would take her elsewhere or get her where she was.... It was Toni.... Meriwether was with her, at her side, holding her hand, watching her flushed face.... But she couldn't imagine her with a man, not Rafe, not Warren or Nathan...nor with a woman. Every time a fantasy took shape it vaporized, a vague imprint on an anonymous bed, on a grassy hillside. She couldn't imagine anything any more, least of all herself.

All she wanted now was to get it over.

He tried to keep her hand away, but she had him, stroking his testicles.

It was over.

They lay there quietly.

And then it slipped in off the blind side.

The dog was barking again—and there, suddenly, it was.

Like a cat it jumped up out of nowhere inside her, arching her back, stretching her limbs. There it was in her hands, and she was stroking it. She could feel herself purring. She rolled over on top of him, but instead of spreading her legs she spread his, mounting him as though she were the man. Neither of them knew what she was doing at first, awkwardness, giggling, flinching, shifting of parts.

What's going on, he said.

Shut up, she said, I want to fuck you.

Go right ahead, he said.

And he took her as though he were the woman, wrapping his legs around her back.

I'm going to do it to you right in your tight little ass, she told him.

She let her hair fall, shaking it in his face, buried her mouth in his wild beard, biting his nose, his cheek, his ear, talking dirty.

He had never been entered before—he tensed up. But she kept after him, telling him to relax, to relax—and she was gathering him, he was coming around. She rolled over on her back, turning him around, pulling his buttocks to her face. He thought she wanted him down on her, but what she wanted was to put her tongue in him. For a while, hovering above her, his head cocked as though he were listening to something behind him, he seemed unable to believe what she was doing. Then he began to moan. He fell slowly forward, spreading his cheeks, moaning. Soon her body was quivering, asking for him.

And then, where she had been: a deep heaving inside, her body, body—no longer even hers.

When it was over, she went straight to sleep, and stayed there for several minutes. Then came back out again—and there he was.

"Jesus Christ," Nathan said, beaming, "what happened?"

She smiled and patted his chest, refusing to talk—silently moved him out of the way and went into the bathroom. He wanted to be given credit, or to give it, to reduce "what happened" to their marriage; she wanted to quit lying, not just to him but to herself. When she returned to bed she snuggled up beside him and told him that she might not want to make love again for a long time—if that was all right. He laughed, taking it as a compliment, and said that whatever she wanted was fine with him.

The next morning she experienced pain urinating, a burning. Back suddenly straight, motionless, she broke out in a sweat. For a long time she sat there as though hypnotized, breathing, staring off into space. Finally she broke loose, shuddering violently, and buried her face in her hands. Sweating profusely now, she wept.

She had betrayed everything that Toni stood for and was and that she herself aspired to.

All her lies had indeed come true!

It served her right for fooling with Bobo.

It served her right for not trusting Toni.

How did Toni know?

She had to quit thinking of herself as guilty of something, that was what men wanted you to think. She had done nothing wrong, nothing!

Was it wrong to want to be happy?

The whole thing was frightening.

It wasn't V.D., Toni said so. She said it was psychosomatic.

How did she know?

She couldn't *know!*

But she did.

Toni was right, sex messed everything up.

If it was a message it wasn't telling her that she was guilty, it was telling her that Toni *knew!*

When she finally found her friend later that day her worst fears were confirmed—Toni acted as though she already knew that she had been betrayed. A panic hit Meriwether. She had been trying to think of some way to tell her what had happened without apologizing for it, or some way to apologize for it without misrepresenting it. But now she could not find a way to tell her even about the infection. They were standing side by side on the flagstone terrace, staring out across the field. Toni was preoccupied, aloof to the point of condescension, and she was making no effort to hide it. Meriwether could think of nothing to say, nothing—it all seemed to serve her so perfectly right.

"For godsakes, *say* something, will you? *Please*!"

"Have you seen it?" Toni asked her.

"Seen what?"

She led Meriwether into the dining room and up to the bulletin board and stood in front of it without a word—as though what they were there to see would declare itself.

Which, after a moment, happened: on a piece of scrap paper, written in pencil:

> All interested parties
> Let it be known
> Makar Atnui Aknada
> died 20 July
> & was reborn
> Solcuni Oroko Macchu
> 21 July 1969

"What does that mean?" Meriwether asked.

Toni shrugged, not at the note but at the question—as if to say that anybody who had to ask would never know.

The likes of Makar Atnui Aknada was far beyond Meriwether now, much less Solcuni Oroko Macchu. She fell to mouthing cliches of awe at Makar's latest far-out move. Toni's attention wandered—until soon Meriwether's humiliation was complete.

As out of it, she said to herself later, as Nathan—bracing for the real depression that she knew would come.

Two days later there appeared on the board another notice.

Cum if u can
Poetree Reading
Works of Joseph Mana
and Makar Atnui Aknada
read by
Solcuni Oroko Macchu
Franklin House
8 p.m.

Everybody was there, even Toni. It turned out to be the most formal occasion of the summer, no cats or dogs or wood carving or letter writing during the performance. It was the first time since "Pluto" that they had all been together, and it was the last. Solcuni was dressed not in a brightly colored robe but in a white shirt, open at the collar, blue gabardine pants, low-cut black shoes, dark rayon socks, and his hair was done up in pigtails, each bowed off with a tiny pink ribbon. A more or less ordinary life-size black man halved out in the middle between a freak and a clerk: an assistant professor of something in a tenure track somewhere. In place of the corduroy bag he even had an old worn-out briefcase, collapsed along the top, Joseph Mana's initials flaking off around the lock.

The reading came out of the briefcase: no aints and funny numbers and weird spit-sucking laughs: his diction was perfect—you would have known that he was black but not from the South. And he read with a professional respect for the text, a classically controlled and modulated voice, full of feeling but no pyrotechnics. The early poems were political, an angry Black in white America, literate, articulate, accessible, the sort of thing the *Times* would acknowledge; and the later, though harder to follow—love poems to Black Woman, incanta-

tions to a mythic goddess—were still perfectly intelligible, even political themselves in the broadest sense of the word.

Everybody thought that they understood what was going on for a
change. Although Makar as most of them had known him had not
written those poems, they wanted to think that he had. They wanted
to believe that all that mojo had been merely a smoke screen for an
angry Black they could understand and applaud. Even Nathan, who
should have known better by now, thought that the war on ignorance
and arrogance had been won, that Makar Atnui Aknada was indeed
dead, and that a new man stood, white shirt and pink ribbons, to
honor him.

As running commentary between the poems, Solcuni talked about
Makar in the third person, supplying the information he had refused
to divulge all summer. He told them that Makar had grown up in a
small black community outside Lexington, Kentucky called Jimtown.
That his father had been a handyman for the same white family all his
life—gardener, chauffeur, cook, butler, and nursemaid to the grand-
children who looked on him as a father, and on the young Makar,
known then as Frankie Jackson, as a brother—until his father was
accused of stealing a gun and fired. That he was one of seven children,
the oldest, all the rest girls, plus his mother's sister who lived with
them. That his father, after he was fired, spent most of his time fishing,
sitting quietly in a flat-bottom boat on the creek watching a cork as
though it were the only thing in the world worth paying any attention
to. That as a child he used to play with the bait boxes and bumper
jacks in the rumble seat of his father's old Ford and imagine sleeping
there in order to escape the house full of women. That he left Jimtown
when he was seventeen, worked his way through a B.A. and an M.A.
at Howard and another M.A. at Columbia playing the piano, toward
the end with Charlie Mingus. And on and on, piling up the facts.
Everything they had all summer wanted to know about Makar, Solcuni told them. In the end, however, it all seemed less important than
they would have thought, considerably less important—which Solcuni made a point of telling them he had known all along.

"Is that what you want to know? You can tell what's underneath by
looking at what's on the surface—is that what you're saying? Nothing
but pets in your permanent community?" He chuckled, putting the
poems back in the briefcase, and with them his reading voice. "I've
heard that."

Franklin House was silent, no one moved, they all watched him. It had been that way from early on, a steady deepening of attention throughout the room, the inescapable emergence of something like tenderness toward him. Had he stopped there, it probably would have swelled up into applause, sustained—asking him to bow.

"I've heard that one," he went on, a trace of the old tease back in his voice. "Talking about the food chain? It's a chain all right, ain't nobody going to argue with you about that. Everything's always after something to eat. Frankie's daddy knew that. They said he stole their gun. He knew all about something to eat, Frankie's daddy did. He could sit there and watch that cork all day. Something down there nibbling all the time. Like the Friday-night meetings—you know what I mean? What's-his-name there and the money," he said, pointing at Nathan with a big grin, and then at Toni, "What's-her-name and the permanent revolutionary community. Ain't nobody going to argue about that. Trouble is, it don't account for song. Food and money's all in the daytime, you know what I mean? It's all in the daytime. Still don't answer the question about what happens in the dark. Lots of folks carrying on about where they come from. Out of Jimtown, and Jimtown out of slavery, and slavery out of Africa. Going from New Jersey over to Africa. If that's as far as you're going you might as well stay right where you are. Don't have to go to Africa for that. Go looking for it, freedom ain't what you find. Africa come out of the waters, and the waters come out of that up there," he said, indicating the heavens. "There's your song. There's your permanent community. Ain't a pet in it. Talk to the sharks about food, about good and evil. Africa ain't far enough back, you know what I mean? Africa just another flat-bottom.... "

All the time Solcuni was talking, Medders was inching toward him, a pocket of restlessness in the middle of the still room. Toni was sitting with her back to the wall staring out the window—she didn't move. Rafe, who seemed to be watching Solcuni, didn't move either, but he too was aware now of everything that Warren did. Medders had that look he got, detached, haughty, itching to say something. Others in the room were becoming aware of something too, the re-emergence of old griefs.

Solcuni, gathering his things together, appeared to be getting ready to quit the podium—

"What *does* happen in the dark?" Medders asked him.

Toni looked at her husbnd as though she thought she should be angry. It was as though he had pointed a cryptic finger, and there at the

end of it was a daemon. First herself—then immediately Solcuni. The
question transformed him into an angry Cupid, pink ribbons and all.
Fascinated now, she watched: except for Rafe, who had turned to look
at Medders, everyone watched it happen: dancing over to Medders,
Solcuni shot him in the eyes with his attention.

"Un-huh un-huh. It do for a fact. In the dark it love to happen," he
said, bounding away, his black-shoed feet unavoidably angry now.
Although Toni and Rafe were the only ones who had any idea what
was going on, everybody knew for certain now that something was—
yet again for the first time. Solcuni was in stride, putting one black
shoe in front of another, saying, "That's a good question you got
there. The only thing about it that ain't good is you—you know what I
mean? I mean you and the question ain't in the same movie. The
question belongs with this one right here." He was with Nathan now,
calling attention to his broad chest, his large strong body. "On
account of, it's his question, you know what I mean? He really do
want to know—rest of you just think you do. On account of, he knows
now about not knowing. Am I right? Dark ain't about to happen in
most movies?"

"You're right," Nathan said.

"If it's your question, then by god ask it!"

"What *does* happen in the dark?" Nathan said.

"You asking me?"

"I thought so."

"I reckon you did." Solcuni whirled around, delivering his answer
to Medders. "Some folks tell you, run a flat-bottom at night, you find
out what's there, like a nigger. But that's just folks talking. Flat-
bottom itself change things, you know what I mean? I mean there ain't
but one person here who's enjoying this." He delivered everyone's
attention to Toni: from her place against the wall, back straight, wide
eyes clear and unblinking, she was watching him, obviously with great
pleasure. "And she ain't the one it's meant for," taking everyone back
to Nathan. "Nigger don't know nothing but what jumps up on a
nigger in the dark. Plenty of white folks know that. All kinds of stuff
don't know a flat-bottom, or don't care, jump right up on it in the
dark. But lots of stuff do. Lots of stuff stay out of sight, even to a
nigger. Run all night and still ain't into the dark. Camp what's-
its-name—people talking to people about people. And you ain't no
different," he told Medders, pointing all five fingers at him, "you just
think you are. Who's winning and what happens next—don't know

nothing but what the world's like with you in it, as the resident composer. Like knowing money and sex without knowing song."

"You're still not answering the question," Medders said.

"You're still not asking it," Solcuni said.

"Isn't it all one thing?" Jerry said, first to one of them and then the other. "Isn't this the song too? Here, now?"

"Why do you always have to threaten us," Medders said. "If not with your fists, then your anger. I always end up feeling jacked around."

"When all you want to be is jacked-off? If you're Cupid, that's one thing, but I thought that was the role you was trying to give me, big bow at the end. I'm going to show you your role." He returned to Nathan, introducing him, with an elegant gesture, to Toni. "Makar always wanted youall to meet someday. One bunch tell him he betray his race, the other he don't know his place. It's the same thing. Come around telling him the man in the big house is crazy when all they want is to be just like him. No better idea of revolution than I been hearing ain't nothing but pet food—end up jacking-off all the time."

"End up being lectured to, is more like it," Medders said.

"End up forgetting a whole lot of things—you know what I mean? I mean there's better ways to keep from being deprived than sitting around making up lists of things you want—and calling it freedom. Freedom's just another word for nothing left to lose, you know what I mean? I mean you might know the words but you don't know the song. We'll see who knows his place. Ain't got nothing to do with who's winning and what happens next."

"Isn't it all one thing?" Jerry kept saying, and each time more people would agree with him. Even Nathan was nodding his head, agreeing to anything except what was happening.

"Trouble with that is," Solcuni told him, refusing to let him off that easy, "circle don't exist till something's outside it. Ask what's-her-name—you ain't never going to see her nodding. You don't know you got a stomach till there's something wrong with it. Ask this one," he said, presenting Meriwether, introducing her to Nathan. "You want to know what's happening in the dark—here it is. Makar always thought of youall as married, you know what I mean? I mean I'm going to tell you about married. When you're inside there ain't no outside, ain't no chorus—there ain't even no inside. There's your one thing, your here and now. Ain't nobody winning. Ain't no next. You're a long way from the one thing when you go to talking about it.

The chorus ain't the play, you know what I mean? All a circle tells you is where you're looking at it from."

"Bug off, Frankie," Medders told him. "You got to stand *some*where! I detect someone trapped again in his metaphor."

"On account of you got a bunch of words in your head? A bunch of corks bobbing? How you going to stand somewhere with your toes being nibbled? Ask the boss there about standing somewhere with your toes being nibbled. You afraid, just like the rest of them—except you want to act like you don't know it. A man don't own nothing, you know what I mean? Start thinking of it as an ox and it's going to get gored, end up fighting and arguing all the time, tapping your watch and telling people something's wrong. There's something wrong all right, but it ain't what happens in the dark. The price tag's still hanging off your robe, and you don't know it. Where *you* been—that's the question. Rehearsing is where you been, angry at me for not going with you. Don't talk to me about threatening. Every idea you got's about something that's gone, nothing but words in your mouth. I'll show you how to act like you ain't been cuckolded. Don't talk to me about permanent community till you're ready to talk song."

"You're saying it's possible to live outside history," Medders said. "That's bullshit."

"There's your history," he said, presenting Toni to him. "There's everybody's history. Now let's hear you talk. Bullshit is what you were saying."

"Leave me out of it," she said.

"You just did," Solcuni told her. "Too far out to go looking. Am I right, boss?" he turned to Nathan.

"You got me!" Nathan laughed.

"Not yet," Solcuni said. "Later. Unless of course you're still living outside history where it's all one thing. You got to look out for them people, you know what I mean? I mean you ain't had a stomach ache till you been lectured to about history—and her sitting right here in the room. I mean, there ain't nobody here that I can see, just what's fate-fucked. Am I right?" he called to Rafe—who gave him the peace sign. "I'm human too—is that what kind of shit this place wants me to say? Wants me to act like I ever said anything different? You was talking about lectures, well here it is. All history just another flat-bottom, bunch of corks bobbing. You was talking about being got, well here it is. Ain't nothing real till everything is. You was afraid of Makar, just like you still afraid. And that's a fact—there's your song.

That's what happens in the dark. You ain't going to hear it in African robes unless you can hear it right here."

"Exactly!" Jerry said. "Right here, right now!"

"A body'd end up curious what it is you hear."

"The song!"

"What I hear is bullshit. People saying leave me out of it. Talking about history like there was somewhere else to be. That's what I hear. People afraid of their lives, afraid of dying."

"Do you really believe that you can carry no more baggage than that?" Medders asked him.

"Un-huh. Un-huh. You done found your question—is that what you're saying? You might of done it—I'm going to answer your question. Don't come around here talking about the heart of darkness if all you got to say is the horror, the horror. That's fair, ain't it? No better idea of history than you got, might as well be politics. Might as well be sociology. Them's all just lists, just lists. I been on too many lists already —you understand what I'm saying? End up thinking you're going to win the war on ignorance by knowing things. Lists of oxes and how they got gored. Song goes right on past the shriveled heads, hardly even notice—right on out the other side of words. Anybody been to the moon tell you you ain't going to get there in no spaceship. Want to go where you ain't been before you got to forget Hershey bars. That's your idea of history, not mine. Long as you taking Walter Cronkite you ain't going nowhere. Ain't no astronaut going to put his foot down on the moon till he gives up the idea of coming back, you know what I mean? I mean your idea of baggage and mine ain't the same. You ain't going nowhere as long as you thinking all the time about coming back. Ain't no coming back in the food chain."

"Just money, sex and song?" Jerry said.

"Ain't no astronaut going to step down on the moon, all he's going to step down on is the sole of his foot. And if he knew that," Solcuni said, lifting his foot from the seat of the folding chair where it had been resting, the black shoe. He put his foot down firmly, saying "he'd already be there."

With that it was obvious he was done. Although he stayed there at the podium for another two or three minutes, staring out the window —already he seemed far away. No one spoke, no one watched him. Pulling a blue handkerchief from his back pocket and picking up his briefcase, Solcuni left without looking at anyone, pausing at the door briefly to wipe his face. They heard the screen door slam, heard

Nietzsche hit his head on the fender as he scrambled out from under the van; and, seeing who it was, bark only once. All eyes were still averted. The feeling was, the old feeling: a wonderful thing had somehow ended badly.

At dinner Medders informed Nathan that he was quitting his teaching job to devote himself to the possibilities of a permanent community at Farmington. And later that night Nathan got a call from California telling him that Ortega had been sent home from the hospital; they gave him a month to live, at the most three.

The trustees met in Franklin on a Saturday morning three weeks later, eight days before the end of the session, and dismissed out of hand a carefully prepared proposal, presented by Medders, to turn Farmington into a year-round community. Where was the money coming from, the trustees kept asking—from a commitment to finding it, they kept being told. When the president asked Medders to withdraw the proposal for the time being and to take a seat on the board, he walked out of the meeting, followed by Toni, Rafe, Bobo, Rhonda and several others. And finally by Meriwether.

Everyone stayed on at Farmington until the end, but the atmosphere was subdued at best, and at worst full of resentment and accusation. Despite the widespread disillusionment, few were ready to go back where they came from. Their lives had been changed that summer more deeply than any of them yet knew, and in more ways. Nathan, doing what he could to conciliate, got permission from the board to keep the place open two weeks into September. Warren had nowhere to go now, and the extra days were welcomed by others too. Nathan himself dreaded returning to Cambridge. And it helped preserve some semblance of community through the rest of the regular session—they had to decide how to run the kitchen without a cook, how to handle the added expense of keeping the place open, what sort of rules in general would govern. Nathan insisted on only one thing: that he have no more responsibility than anyone else. The twenty-one people who stayed claimed to understand what that meant and all of them agreed to it.

When the community closed formally, Nathan left Farmington to Meriwether and Medders and went back to Cambridge for a couple of days to tend to business. He wandered through their house as though it belonged to someone else, opening closets and drawers. He did not have the slightest idea where his marriage was or even how to try to find out. He sat around in a stupor, unable to remember what he had come to do, listening to the news every hour. He went to school, hoping that his business there would take hold of him. Which it did, after its fashion—he walked right into the middle of the latest tenure and promotion intrigue. A few hours among his colleagues and he was seriously considering resigning. He kept thinking about Medders. About living at Farmington year-round himself. About what a relief it would be not to have to apologize for his life any longer. He found himself telling a colleague that he could just as easily teach Bach or baseball now as photography, it made no difference—he taught himself. Medders had told him that once. And he had thought it was irresponsible. Just as the colleague did, who demanded to know what in the hell had happened to him. Meriwether had learned how to stick her tongue up his ass—that's what he should have said. He could not face going back to the house. He went to Harvard Square and ate alone, reading *The New York Times*. He could feel himself being drawn back into that world. He thought about going to the library. He thought about going to a movie. He walked down Mass. Ave. looking in the windows. He had a cup of coffee and smoked a cigarette. At a payphone he called Farmington collect. No one answered. The phone rang and rang. He could not understand it. He asked the operator to break the connection and start all over again. Still no one answered. What was going on? He got in his car, listened to the news, and then sat there for a long time with no idea what to do next. He went to see friends, hoping to talk about Meriwether, but there was no way. He tried to tell them about Solcuni Oroko Macchu, alias Makar Atnui Aknada, and they laughed and said how *aw*ful. Was it *all* that bad? Her name was Martha. She was an interior decorator. Her husband, Ken, was an English professor. They were Nathan and Meriwether's oldest and closest friends in Cambridge. They wanted to talk about I.F. Stone and the war. Nathan used their phone to call Farmington again. Still no answer. He called California and talked to Ortega's wife. He told her that he would try to come out there before school started. She asked him how Meriwether was. He said that she was fine. She told him that he would have to come soon if he wanted to see Ortega alive. He thought of asking Martha if he could stay there for the night. She told her big story of the summer. She had taken the children swimming and had had a heat stroke. I thought I was on another planet, she said. I thought I could climb up on top of the house and fly off. I kid you not. I was ab-so-*lute*ly terrified, out of my *mind!* And Kenneth was worse. I've never had a drug in my life, but I'm sure I've tripped now. Nathan asked her what happened, and she said that she had taken two libriums instead of one and within an hour she was all right.

He was back in Cambridge all right.

He went home and slept on the couch.

As soon as Nathan left Farmington three of Rafe's friends from Boston appeared, a couple with another big dog, and a bare-foot long-haired guy with blue sunglasses. In the back of their van, covered with a tarp, were two old wood burning stoves, laid side by side with a chair cushion between them. And a chain saw. Without bothering to meet anybody they helped themselves to the food and to the accommodations. They took soup from the stove, cottage cheese from the refrigerator, vegetables from the garden, they did not wash their dishes, and they let the dog run loose in the kitchen and dining room, terrorizing the cats. Everybody was furious, but no one said anything to them, or to Rafe and Toni. Those who could get along without the kitchen and the dining room withdrew, and those who could not made do. No one was willing to take charge. The rumor was that more of Rafe's friends were on the way, that they were going to hole up in Van Velder for the winter. No one could quite believe it—or disbelieve it either. The situation got so bad that finally a meeting was arranged on the lawn at Franklin. Toni refused to have anything to do with it, but Rafe showed up, listening to all the complaints with a smirk.

"You know what I hear?" he told them. "I hear a lot of bullshit is what I hear."

"You've got nothing but contempt for us," Suzie said. "You and Toni both! You're trying to take the place over!"

Solcuni, who had just wandered into the meeting, chuckled—and wandered back out.

"You've got nothing but contempt for yourself is where it's at," Rafe said. "A whole lot of paranoid bullshit."

With that he got up and walked off, leaving an imprint in the grass.

And leaving the rest of them, their arms wrapped around their knees, squinting at one another in the sunlight.

Sharon was crying. "That sonofabitch! That sonofabitch!"

"I guess we'll have to wait until Nathan gets back," Jerry said.

The feeling was, they were being driven out. Some were already thinking of leaving.

There was an eerie stillness attending everything, rooms empty, doors standing open, chairs turned abruptly away from tables, instant coffee left uncapped on the stove, week-old newspapers scattered about like collapsing tents, silence. There was not a human sound anywhere. He hurried upstairs to their room. Her clothes were gone. The crib was still there, and the child's things, but hers were gone.

She had run off with Medders—he was sure of it. Or Toni.

But where was Mason?

He rushed back downstairs and out the door and down the drive toward David and Ellie's.

There Medders was coming across the field from the Music Shed with Mason on his shoulders.

"Daddy!"

Warren put the child down and he ran full-tilt into Nathan's arms. "What the hell's going on?"

"Same old shit," Warren said. "Everything. Nothing."

"Where's Meriwether?"

"On her way back."

"On her way back from where?"

"Vermont."

Vermont meant her parents.

"Why didn't she take Mason?"

"She found out that Toni's been fucking Solcuni and she lost it. She's all right now. She called last night."

"Toni and Solcuni?! Good God! Oh Christ!" Then, almost immediately, "Of course!"

"You got it," Medders said.

"Guess what!" Mason said. "Warren let me sleep in his bed with him!"

Word got around quickly that Nathan was back and within the hour everyone except Rafe and Toni and Solcuni were on the sunporch, filling him in. Although Rafe's friends were gone, at least for the time being, everyone agreed that since that meeting on the lawn things had gone from bad to worse. They were all depressed, nobody wanted to go near Van Velder, everybody blamed Toni and Rafe.

Nathan was poised to take the situation into his own hands when Meriwether returned. Without even looking at him she slipped into the room and took a seat at the table, crossing her arms over her chest. And suddenly he was right back where he had always been, confined to what he thought she would approve of. She was angry, there was no question about that—but at what or whom he could not tell.

Once she got the drift of the discussion she said, "Either they leave or I do."

That was almost too good for Nathan to believe. To him it sounded as though she was putting their marriage first again—or at least might be.

When they finally got to a vote only two people did not know where they stood: fourteen of the sixteen there wanted to ask them to leave.

Only it was not *them* any more, it was just Rafe.

Warren had managed to separate them, more by his presence than anything he said.

Nathan balked at that, convinced that Rafe was little more than a pawn. Unable to press the point alone, however, he ended up going along.

"Okay," he said, stating his reservations one last time in the tone of his voice. "But let's get this straight. We're going to meet with Rafe for the purpose of presenting a community decision to him as a community, and to give him a chance to ask questions and speak his piece, but *not* for the purpose of *deciding* anything—right?"

"Oh come on!" Meriwether said. "Nobody wants to do this!"

"Exactly. That's why I want it to be absolutely clear what we're doing. I'm the one who always gets left holding..."

"The decision is already made!" several people assured him.

"*Okay!*" He jumped up so quickly he knocked his chair to the floor. "Let's get this over with!"

At first Rafe refused to have anything to do with a meeting, cursed the very idea, and cursed Nathan, whom he accused of having become a "trustee"—and then, after talking privately with Toni, he consented, on the condition that Solcuni be present. Nathan agreed to that, though he did not like it, and the meeting was arranged for eight that night at Franklin.

Rafe was one of the first there, accompanied by Toni, and they took seats without speaking to anyone—Rafe cockily in the rocker next to the fireplace—Toni all the way across the room, half hidden behind a pillar, by herself. She looked ravaged, as though she had not slept or bathed in days. People filed in, one and two at a time, talking quietly, smiling timidly at each other, avoiding her, trying to conceal their excitement. When everyone was seated they waited, virtually in silence, for Solcuni. Finally someone went after him—but he stayed only long enough to see the proceedings under way, then left, appearing bored.

What Nathan feared most was compromise, and the room was full of it. But right from the start Rafe himself precluded the possibility. When told that he was being asked to leave he said "Why?" as though he could not imagine.

One after another people repeated what they had said in the earlier meeting, testifying at length to his abusive treatment, several with deep feeling, two in tears. Rafe sat there throughout without saying a word, his head laid back on the high back of the rocker in a posture that was hard to read—maybe it was contempt, maybe exhaustion; he gave the impression that he himself no longer knew, no longer even cared.

Finally someone asked him, "What have you got to say about all this?"

"I haven't got anything to say—this is your movie, not mine."

"Will you leave?"

"No," he said.

"Why?"

"Why should I?"

"Because we're asking you to!"

"We don't do things that way around here," Rafe said, looking straight at Nathan. "This is as much my place as it is yours—right, Professor?"

"The rules are changing," Nathan said. "Tonight."

"You know what this is?" Rafe said. "This is a witch hunt."

"What does *that* mean?" Medders demanded.

"It means it's your problem, not mine," Rafe said.

Solcuni reappeared, as though *witch hunt* were his cue. Carrying a cup of tea he sat down on the steps behind Rafe, head bowed, chuckling.

Everything began to shift under foot.

Solcuni and Toni in the same room together made many of them uncomfortable now, especially Nathan. *How predictable* was what they had all said—though none had predicted it. Like a loaded gun behind the pillar over there, Toni was sitting bolt upright on a folding chair, gripping with both hands the seat between her knees, a look of great pain on her face, her eyes closed much of the time—nothing predictable about her at all, except that all along she had meant what she said, exactly. Everyone in the room knew that Camp Farmington was now armed, that indeed the excitement was over—or perhaps just beginning.

"Well we're making it your problem too, Rafe," Nathan told him. "I'm getting just a little tired of everything being our problem and not yours. The idea here is, we're all in it together."

"That's right," Rafe said. "So if I have to leave, everybody else has to leave too. You'll have to get the cops to throw me out if you want me to leave."

"That's what you want, isn't it?" Medders said.

"You haven't the slightest idea what I want, Warren Medders, and you never will."

"Well what do you want?" somebody asked.

"At the moment I'd like very much for you people to take some time off from examining me and examine yourself for just a little while."

"What is it that you see that we don't?" Nathan asked.

"I haven't the slightest idea what you see, believe me. What I see is a bunch of uptight housewives. You're all panicked because you're headed back to the suburbs, and you're looking for a scapegoat. Well you can look somewhere else, because I'm not going to play that game."

Solcuni was chuckling again, the old hook in their juices, the sound of something being sucked away.

They wanted him to leave.

Nathan especially wanted him to leave.

Nobody said anything to him, but they were all thinking that they would be a lot better off if he would leave.

And so he did. As quietly as he came, as though to show them how wrong they were, he stood up and turned around and walked out.

There was big hole in the middle of everything now, something spinning down, like a lighted match being sucked into a gas tank.

"I don't understand how you can stay when you know you're not wanted!" Meriwether said.

"There are a whole lot of things you don't understand!"

"Fuck you, Rafe!"

"Fuck *you*, Meriwether!"

"Okay, okay," Nathan said, relieved to see such bad feeling between them, "knock it off!"

"Let's take a break," someone suggested.

"No, we're going to finish this, right now," Nathan said.

"You afraid to give people a chance to think about what they're doing?" Rafe asked.

"Okay, we'll *take* a break!" Nathan said. "But I've got something to say first. I want one thing to be clear. The community is asking you to leave. You can leave quietly, like the community wants you to, or you can defy the community, as you seem intent on doing. But if you do you've still got me to deal with. And I'm going to *tell* you to go. Is that clear? The only choice you got is *how* you're going to leave."

"You'll have to call the cops, " Rafe said.

"No, I won't," Nathan said.

There was a long, uneasy silence, the two of them staring at one another.

Rafe asked for a show of hands—just who was it that wanted him to leave.

It was a shrewd move.

There was no way Nathan could object.

Only twelve people were counted. Of the remaining nine, eight now wanted him to stay, including three who had testified against him.

And there was one abstention—Meriwether.

At the break Nathan bolted through the door, grabbing the first thing he could get his hands on, an old window screen that was leaning against the house. He smashed it to pieces against a tree. Then took off running up the road.

He felt that she had set him up. That the whole situation had been rigged to prove he was a fascist.

Well maybe he was.

He did not regret anything that he had said or done—the prospect of being free of all those people and their interminable pulling and pushing was the most exciting thing he had felt in a long time.

Maybe the best thing in the world for him and Meriwether would be to get shut of one another. Whatever the hell she wanted it was obviously beyond him. He had tried and he had tried and he had tried, and the harder he tried the more impossible it got. It was humiliating, and he was done being humiliated.

He wished that Solcuni had stayed. He wished that Solcuni had seen him draw the line. Seen somebody in that miserable place quit acting miserable.

It seemed inevitable to him now that it was Rafe and not Toni they were dealing with. Nobody had been able to face anything clearly all summer. It was the story of the whole community from conception on, dealing with one thing in terms of another. Maybe it wasn't even Toni they should be dealing with, but Solcuni.

How then could he throw Rafe out?

With his bare hands, with a vengeance, that's how!

So much for their little idea of a self-structuring community, so much for fairness and decency and justice. It was not ignorance and arrogance he was declaring war on, it was frustration and impotence. It was misery.

When he dealt with Medders he acted like a professor. When he dealt with a professor he acted like Medders. When he dealt with Meriwether he acted like.... There was no name for it. It was craven, disgusting. Misery was what she did to him, what he did to himself because of her, what they did to each other.

And all of it in the name of love.

Maybe it wasn't even Solcuni he wanted in that seat, but Meriwether. He didn't want to crack her skull, that wasn't it. He wanted her to know what a miserable self-indulgent castrating bitch she was. He wanted to make her feel what it was like to be married to her.

He wished that Solcuni had been there when he told Rafe what was going to happen.

Maybe Solcuni was the one they were dealing with after all. Maybe he *was* in that seat and they didn't even know it. Or maybe it was Toni McHugh.

When Nathan got back to Franklin he found Meriwether talking privately to Toni in his office. And in the kitchen he found David talking quietly to Rafe, trying to explain the way he had voted.

The tension was gone, everything had changed.

It appeared that the expulsion had been rescinded, that indeed the situation was in his lap.

Well, there it was—finally. There he was, there they all were. Now they would find out once and for all how Farmington really worked.

But then he discovered that Rafe had agreed to go, that he and Toni were leaving as soon as they could.

He caught Meriwether alone and asked her what had happened.

"What happened to what?" she snapped back.

"Why did you change your mind?"

"Did you know that Toni's got a massive urinary tract infection and is in such pain she can barely talk? She hardly knows what happened in there tonight!"

"Is that why you changed your mind?"

"You have no right whatsoever to judge them. You never even talked to them. You never even went down to the projection room. And then you started threatening Rafe. No sir. *You're* the one who changed people's minds. You wanted to throw Toni out, but you didn't have the balls. You didn't throw Makar out, you're not going to throw Toni out. Not as long as I'm here you're not."

He wanted to say well then he would throw the whole lot of them out. "You hate me, don't you?"

"No, I don't. I pity you."

They were staring at one another.

She was standing beside a lamp in his office, the light full in her face. It scared him what he saw there, the disgust. He could hardly look at her.

"I pity us both, and I'm sick of it."

Well there it was—finally.

"Then where are we?" he asked.

"It won't work."

"Where does that leave us?"

"I don't know."

"Let's take Mason to your mother's and go to California together. We've got to get out of this place. We haven't got a chance in the world here. We haven't been alone together in months."

"No," she said.

"It's done awful things to both of us."

"You still don't know what's happened, do you?"

He wanted to mash her face into a pulp—maybe that's what she was talking about. "Where do you want to go then?"

"I don't want to go anywhere. I want to stay right here. I'm going to have Van Velder winterized and stay right here."

"Nobody's staying here!" he said. "I'm closing Farmington down! Just as goddamn fast as I can!"

She gave him another of those looks.

"Just try!" she said.

She turned around and walked off.

"I thought you said she was beyond sex!" he called after her.

Meriwether spun around, her face distorted, near tears. "You're awful! You're as awful as he is! You're all disgusting!"

"I'm just repeating what you told me."

"He treated her like shit. It was rape!"

"The second time? And the third and the fourth?"

"You don't understand anything! You never will!"

This time she ran.

He wanted to take back what he had said—but she was gone.

So he was the one who was being kicked out of the community. It wasn't Rafe or Toni or Meriwether or Solcuni at all, but he himself they had been dealing with.

When he got upstairs he found Mason standing up in his crib crying. The child had thrown everything out, all his toys were scattered around the room, and he was leaning on the rail exhausted and hoarse. There was no telling how long he had been screaming.

"Oh sweet child!" He lifted him out and hugged him. "Daddy's sorry!" He hugged him tightly, back and forth. "Daddy's sorry! It won't ever happen again! Never again as long as I live!"

After Mason was asleep Nathan called the president of the board and told him what had happened with Rafe and Toni. Told him that he was shutting the place down, that if Meriwether or Medders called to tell them Farmington was closed until the trustees opened it again in the spring. The next day, however, he called back and told him that the money had been found to winterize, that henceforth Medders and Meriwether were in charge: whatever they wanted had his backing. He was on his way to California with Mason, and he was not returning.

In their first act as the new co-directors of Farmington, Meriwether and Medders excluded Solcuni from consideration—on Toni's behalf. Inauspicious a beginning as it seemed they believed that they had no choice. She did not even have to ask.

No one told him. He found out from a conjunction of numbers on the radio. He shut his eyes and sucked in his stomach and peeled the dashiki off in one continuous motion. Took off the holster, then his shoes, then rolled his pants legs up to the knees. Then stood there in the center of his room with his eyes closed and his arms hanging heavily at his sides, breathing himself down.

Instead of going straight through the graveyard he took to the woods running and completely circled Farmington. He ran to the image of a loose string being dangled and jumped in mid-air, head wobbling, eyes shut most of the way, hands and arms and shoulders and legs loose, dropping the joints out with each stride, a series of muscular collapses smoothed out by the pace. His breathing, high up in the lungs, was quick and explosive, through the nostrils, each exhalation accompanied by a sound, a kind of grunt, as though he were punching a bag. When he came up out of the woods carrying a switch, he was sweating as though he had been in a sauna.

The door to the projection room was cracked to the breeze, a paperback wedged under the corner. Toni was asleep on a mattress in the corner, her back to the door. Rafe, his shirt off and barefoot, was on his hands and knees in the middle of the room, studying the circuitry of a dismantled Carousel. When the dog started barking outside he looked up just in time to see the three-pronged claw-shaped switch slip through the crack in the door—followed by Solcuni glazed with sweat, his pants rolled up to his knees. Rafe grabbed a screw driver and jumped to his feet.

Toni rolled over and sat up abruptly.

Solcuni had his eyes shut and he was running in place and he was whipping himself about the feet and ankles.

"Get out!" she screamed.

"You heard her!" Rafe said. "Get out!"

Toni jumped to her feet—but there was no place to go.

When he turned the switch on her she lunged for the door, but he blocked her, knocking her to the floor. Then grabbed her up by the hair, spinning her like a rope and tearing at her clothes. Rafe tried twice to stop him. The second time Solcuni turned on him briefly and rammed his head into the wall, knocking him momentarily unconscious. When he came to he crawled out the door and ran up the hill, the dog nipping at his heels.

It appeared that Solcuni intended only to switch her. He got her into a corner, X-ing the strokes out broadly, rhythmically—more a drama than a beating. His eyes were shut, each stroke measured to a breath, each breath punctuated with a moan, all the time running in place like a quickened pulse, neat rapid little steps, his bare feet patting the floor —the violence contained. "Un-huh. Un-huh. What makes you think I'd *want* to stay?" But then the switch broke, and broke again, each time closer to flesh on flesh, and then the switch was gone, he was slapping her—and the whole thing turned suddenly brutal. He broke her nose and opened up cuts on her face and head. When Nathan got there she was crumpled up in the corner, unconscious, blood on the walls and floor, and Solcuni was kicking her about the buttocks and thighs with the side of his heel.

For a moment they faced one another across the room, each poised —Nathan enraged, ready to charge—Solcuni suddenly calm, way back, something playful taking hold of him again. That catch-me-if-that's-what-you-think-you're-doing look coming on his face. And then he was out the window and running. And Nathan, leaving Rafe and Meriwether to care for Toni, was after him.

For the first several hundred yards, across the field and into the woods, they sprinted—not all out at first, but soon Nathan was running as fast as he could. The black man never looked back, but every time Nathan picked up the pace, so did he. When to his astonishment he realized that Solcuni was faster than he was, he slowed up, content to wear him out, thinking that that would probably be wiser anyway.

They took to a hillslope, diagonally, kicking down rocks and fallen branches, picked up speed once more along a ridge, and then turned again and ran for over a mile along a stone fence—the black man steadily increasing his lead. Up another hill, and along the ridge, he disappeared momentarily, then reappeared, over to the left a little, still running—still not looking back—then disappeared again. For stretches of time now Nathan was running blindly, no idea where the man was. Then he would reappear, in an unexpected place, the field widening each time. He reappeared down the hill, way up the creek down the hill, standing still now, and facing, as though he were wait-ing, and then gone again. Nathan was tiring, his fury had played out into anger, and his anger was playing out into confusion. Without breaking stride he turned full crazy-kneed circles, loops in a straight line the direction of which was itself arbitrary now. He felt as if he were no longer giving chase but being led—even being chased himself. When Solcuni appeared next, up along the ridge, he was openly play-ing with him, peeking out from behind trees. And when Nathan gained the ridge, he was gone—for longer stretches each time. The last he saw of him was on the far side of a clearing, dancing from tree to tree—then gone, running.

When Nathan finally gave up he was near Diana's Pool. And went on up there to rest.

And there Solcuni was, hunkered down on the flat rock.

He was fully dressed now.

"I been wondering where you was at," he said.

He was in the same spot where he sat that day with elbows on knees and held the gun with both hands in Nathan's face—only now the gun was nowhere in sight, and he was squatted on his heels, close to the edge.

"I been wondering where you was at all sumnmer."

Nathan walked up to him cautiously but without trepidation and knelt down in front of him, a few yards away.

"I want you on the next bus out of here."

"And if I'm not you're going to put me on the one after?"

"That's exactly right."

"And I'll need the help?"

"You'll need the help."

"Un-huh. Un-huh. Listen to him. Come up here to bust ass, put it off on the bus schedule, and then want me to be scared."

"I *would* listen if I were you. I've had it with you."

"No you ain't. You ain't had nothing with nobody. You ain't had nothing with nobody but yourself."

"I'm telling you to get out of here!"

"You a long way from telling me anything. You come up here to bust black ass now bust it."

"There's been enough violence already."

"Un-huh. Un-huh. Enough for you, is that what you mean? Enough till the bus schedule come around? Is that what you mean? We ain't on no bus schedule. I been telling you that all summer, we ain't on no bus schedule. I didn't do nothing to her you wasn't getting ready to do to that kid. Nothing you ain't talking about getting ready to do to me. That's what enough is, huh, what you say it is?"

"But you did it, I didn't. There's a big difference."

"There's a difference all right, but it ain't the one you're talking about. The difference is, you come up here to bust black ass and I ain't going to let you talk your way out of it—that's the difference. I know what you're thinking. You're thinking gun. Ever since you quit thinking this," he said, laying his hand on his skin the way he had done that day in the dining room, "you been thinking this." He pulled the gun out from under the dashiki and held it up with a limp wrist as though it were negligible, dead. "If that's all you thinking you might as well forget that too. That ain't what's going on."

He put the gun down as though he were dialing a number, spinning it across the smooth rock to Nathan, all nines.

It lay there, within easy reach, ringing.

There seemed to be no way Solcuni could get it back.

Nathan stared first at the gun, then at him.

The man was perched precariously on the edge of the rock, asking to be knocked into Diana's Pool.

"Pick it up," he said.

"No," Nathan said. "I don't need a gun. I don't want a gun. That's what I've been trying to tell you."

"You might not want it but you going to need it. Pick the mother-fucker up. Either you going to pick it up with your hand or you going to pick it up with your mouth. I'm telling you—that's the choice you got. The movie done moved out into the parking lot. You been telling me about violence but you don't know violence. You been talking virtue, but you ain't been talking choice. You don't know nothing about what you been telling me."

"You don't frighten me."

"Because you ain't got close enough. If you got close enough you'd be scared. It wouldn't be what you're thinking, evil nigger or power doctor, but you'd be scared."

Nathan picked up the gun.

"That's what you been thinking, ain't it?"

"I been thinking about getting rid of it, if that's what you mean. And that's exactly what I'm going to do."

"You ain't going to get rid of nothing until you get rid of yourself. You ain't got nothing else to get rid of. You going to throw the gun out and feel good, that's all you going to do. That's all you ever going to do. Anything go wrong then, ain't your fault. Some folks it's money or pussy, others it's virtue. Ain't your fault, you a good man. Trouble is, a good man ain't ever going to get rid of nothing, you know what I mean? Too busy holding on. A good man's wife can tell him all about such things, but a good man's trouble is he can't hear. A good man can't hear nothing but himself, because that's all he knows. Which mean he don't even know that. You think you got the gun right there in your hand, just like you think you going to get rid of it—but I got the gun. I still got the gun. It's like everthing else you think. You can't tell what's real from your pecker in your hand. Ain't that what your wife's been trying to tell you?"

"Shut up, Makar," he said calmly.

"It ain't Makar talking."

"Just leave her out of it."

"Un-huh. Un-huh. Here comes the bus. Trouble with that is, I didn't bring her into it. You think I did, but that's just like everything else you think you're telling me, can't tell it from what's in your mouth. And you ain't had nothing real in your mouth, you know what I mean?"

"I'm telling you to shut up. I've had enough of you."

"That's what you think you're telling me. You ain't had nothing in your mouth all summer but yourself, and I've heard enough of it. Ain't that what your woman's telling you? Movie in the projection room now but you ain't got a ticket, big plug stuck up your wish hole? Full of shit till you could bust, and still holding tight?"

Nathan raised the gun and pointed it at him, calmly. "I'm telling you."

"Un-huh. Un-huh. You might just do it—ain't nothing like a good man for telling people things. Here come the bus and Meriwether's driving. We back to Cupid, with a vengeance. I told you about Cupid, didn't I? And you wouldn't listen? Now get a hold of it with both hands, cause I'm going to tell you what she's got in her mouth."

Nathan gripped the gun with both hands and extended his arms out straight, aiming down the barrel at the hairless black chest: midway between the pectorals, halving the distance between the mouth and the belly button: he touched those points as though he were signing the cross, then drew his bead.

"Now sit down and get your knees up. You been asking about my thing, I'm going to tell you about my thing. Get your elbows on your knees. This here's one of them tripod shots, triangulated all the way down."

He did.

He was firmly in place now behind the gun, sighting down the barrel at his mark.

Something wasn't quite right.

He lifted the aim slightly.

There, that was it—in the mouth.

"Un-huh. Un-huh. I see what you mean. It's a vengeance all right. You think you want to leave your woman out of it, is that what you think you want? I'm going to show you what you think you want."

Without taking his eyes off Nathan's he slowly disrobed: first the dashiki, slid it slowly up his back and onto his shoulders: ducked out of it: and tossed it aside: then his shoes and socks: then, still seated, he undid his pants, worked them off, and kicked them aside.

"You ready?"

Slowly he stood up, naked.

It was Nathan's intention to track his mark. Down the barrel he watched Solcuni's face rise up into his neck and his neck up into his chest, into his abdomen — But the gun would not budge — Like a balloon his head expanded, everything began to flip and roll backwards — He shut his eyes.

"Look here!" Solcuni said, cupping his genitals. "Look here!"

But Nathan refused, tightening his grip on the gun, on his eyes, on everything.

"Look here! This what you been thinking! Here's your black skin and your gun, look at it! You don't want to look because you don't want to know. You don't want to know this ain't what you're scared of. That's why you got your eyes shut. You a long way from having your balls cut off, you ain't even got em yet. All you want to know is who's winning and what happens next. I'll tell you who's winning. There's a lot worse things can happen to that white witch than a beating, and one of em is to get away without it. And she knows it. There's the difference you was talking about—*she* knows it and *you*

don't. I'll tell you who's winning. You been playing revolution with a
grown up, thinking it was a kid because you said it was. *She's* winning,
just like she always will. She done took your place away from you and
made you glad to get shut of it. She done took your *wife* away—that's
who's winning. All you got left is a bunch of reasons—why you're
bettern she is, why this, why that. There's a lot worse things you can
do than stomp my ass, and one of em is not to. Lot worse things can
happen to me than get shot by a crazy white man—and one of em is
acting like you know something. You don't know routine from order,
world ain't happened to you yet, just a bunch of ideas about it. World
ain't *ever* going to happen to you, you too busy explaining it. You
think you going to shut your eyes and walk off, but you can't, you ain't
never opened em yet. You can't look at me because you can't look at
yourself. It's your *goodness* you're scared of. There's your violence.
You're *stuck*. All wrapped up in your goodness like a mummy. *There's*
your violence. You're scared of yourself and calling it me, calling it
her. Look here, *here's* where you been all summer, here's where your
woman's been all summer, here's where you all been, and I'm *tired* of
it."

"Shut up, Makar!"

"It ain't Makar talking. I told you. He's dead. How come you can't
listen?"

When Nathan opened his eyes, this is what he saw: Solcuni was
about ten feet away, face on, his knees bent slightly, splayed out, his
feet planted: he was cupping his genitals: his angry face thrust forward: his angry mouth, red, wet: his teeth biting off the last word.
Nathan saw his white teeth flinch, suddenly biting the air—something
hit him, suddenly, inside, deep. Saw his eyes widen, his neck stiffen—a
trace of it hit his knees, they buckled. Nathan saw it surface in a spasm,
rippling outward, snapping his wrists as it left his body—a look of
astonishment on the man's face, then recognition. Nathan saw him
fold inward, sinking to the ground.

He believed that he had shot him.

In horror he watched the man die, then couldn't watch.

When Nathan looked again, Solcuni was standing there: his small
feet neatly together, his knee cocked to hide his sex. He grinned and
curtsied, wrapping his arms around himself as though he were chilly.
He began then to dance.

First his neck came loose, then his head. Then his shoulders and
arms, his hands and legs. He danced loose one joint at a time, as

though he were taking himself apart. He cocked his hips, throwing his sex from one thigh to the other. Then his legs, they snapped out, his knees, his ankles. Soon he was stomping his feet and moaning, gone, on his way into a frenzy.

"Stop it!"

Nathan lurched to his feet slinging the gun toward the river and threw himself headlong at the whirling figure.

Solcuni ducked under and came up: hitting him in the face with his head like a hammer.

The next thing Nathan knew he was lying flat on his back, his face hurt, his head ached, he tasted blood—and the small black man was sitting on his chest, his knees on his shoulders.

"Bus left and we both still here. Ain't no other place to be, I reckon. You all right?"

"I think so," Nathan said.

"Ain't nobody going to know till you do."

"I'm okay."

Solcuni got off and helped him to sit up. Felt his nose to see whether it was broken.

"Sit still for a while, you be all right."

He got dressed, except for the dashiki, which he made into a wet towel for Nathan.

"Thank you."

"It loves to happen."

With his hands behind his head and the cold cloth folded over his face, Nathan lay there quietly on the rock for a long time going over and over what had happened. One thing he knew for sure: he was leaving for California as soon as possible. Occasionally he would ask a question or make a remark, but Solcuni, sitting there next to him with his arms wrapped around his knees, said nothing. Once, without being asked, he took the dashiki back to the river to freshen it. As Nathan's head cleared he talked more and more, expressing his horror at what had happened. To all of them, he said, but most of all to himself. For the first time he truly understood principles: left to instinct he would become, as he had, barbarous. They all would. Whatever the reasons for beating Toni McHugh, whatever the ultimate consequences, it still had to be condemned, without qualification, without apology. "You seem to think you're beyond good and evil," he said at one point, "but I certainly don't. Nobody is. It's one of the most dangerous ideas around." He removed the towel to see how that was being taken. But the man was gone. How long he had been talking to himself he had no idea.

After he got back from the hospital, where Toni was kept for a couple of hours and then released, he went to Solcuni's room to return the shirt in person. His belongings were still there—the next day and the next. But Solcuni never came back. No one ever saw him again.

The dashiki fell thus into Nathan's keeping. He knew what to do with it, or at least what not to do with it—for a while anyway. He took it to California with him, not on the first trip but when he came back a few weeks later to dismantle his darkroom at school and sell the house in Cambridge. Time and again over the next several months he would find it among his things, it would lie awkwardly about for days, then get stuffed back into a closet or a box or a drawer. The next summer the woman he was living with found it in a trunk and wore it over her bikini to the beach. When she saw the pictures he took of her in it, she started wearing it to bed.

The next woman knew what it was without being told (or more exactly what it had become) and sent it, along with several boxes of Mason's outgrown clothes, to the Salvation Army. By then so much grief and bitterness surrounded his experience at Farmington—not just his divorce but a protracted custody fight, which he had won twice but was in the early stages then of losing conclusively—that he was glad to be rid of it. Only once did he try in earnest to set the record straight. It was after a day in court which had gone well for him, toward the end of that first winter. He had Mason, Meriwether was suing for a divorce and custody. No judge would have let her have the child then. For six weeks they had been snowbound; it was all they could do, five of them sleeping around a stove in the dining room, to stay alive. Medders had already left, in protest, the third and last man; Toni was already in effect in charge. Nathan did not need a clincher, but he had it, or thought he did, and he used it, that time and the next: the child's mother was now a lesbian: she and her lover were turning the place into a community of radical feminists: the child would become a political tool. Nathan wanted his woman to know that Farmington was not so simple as she had been hearing it portrayed by his lawyer, nor were any of the people involved—that he felt especially bad hearing Makar described in terms that a judge could understand. They were in a restaurant in San Francisco. Even if he had been a story teller, even if the memory were fresher and his own feelings less tangled, he would never have been able to convey to her what it was like to be around that man. But he tried, that once he really tried. Responding to the intensity in his voice, she listened attentively and made an effort to understand, but she was thirty-six years old, divorced, with two children, and she was tired of what she called "men." He could feel her disconnecting and fading away. Mid-way he broke off, saying that Makar wasn't really what he wanted to talk about—he wanted to talk about them. He believed that they should be thinking about getting married. And so did she. On the way home in the car, her head on his shoulder, her hand on the inside of his thigh, she asked him please to finish the story. When he got to the chase that ended at Diana's Pool, he described himself and Makar as carrying on like a couple of men in a Hollywood movie, oblivious of the fact that Toni could very well have needed their help. When they got home and saw the children to bed, he played the tape for her. He was so far away from it by then he did not realize until the end, when Makar's voice came on *For Nathan...so they say*, that he had played it at the wrong speed. The words were so slurred they were unintelligible. He was relieved to discover that she had fallen asleep. He did not feel good leaving it at that, but everything that he knew now told him that he would be wise to.

After Meriwether extricated herself from Farmington, broke, leaving the place to Toni, she borrowed money from her parents and went back to school to get a teaching certificate. One night at a party, shortly after she moved to Storrs, Connecticut, she walked out on a deck just as it collapsed, falling fifty feet onto the rocky bank of a creek. She appeared in court two weeks later in a back brace. They stopped at nothing in their efforts to discredit her, Nathan and his lawyer, listing all the things that had collapsed out from under her, a woman with an obvious penchant for disaster, managing to hold on to the child that one last time. In her defense she refused to answer their charges—to cooperate, as she put it, with being accused of her life— and refused to have a lawyer; she presented her own case in her own terms, accusing no one of anything. Afterwards she came up to his table to arrange for visits. He stood up, in defense of himself, acting as though he believed every word of his case against her. She sat down, in pain, acting as though they had once been married and had a child still to raise. She frightened him. He thought she was beautiful. He was ashamed of himself. He wondered if she still loved him. He wondered if he still loved her. His new wife was there, seated at the table next to him, watching them both. He did not feel good leaving it at that, but he had grown accustomed to such feelings, even proud of them—impatient with the idea that life was something you were supposed to feel good about.

FICTION COLLECTIVE
Books in Print

Price List:
cloth   paper

	cloth	paper
The Second Story Man by Mimi Albert	8.95	3.95
Althea by J.M. Alonso	11.95	4.95
Searching for Survivors by Russell Banks	7.95	3.95
Babble by Jonathan Baumbach	8.95	3.95
Chez Charlotte and Emily by Jonathan Baumbach	9.95	4.95
My Father More or Less by Jonathan Baumbach	11.95	5.95
Reruns by Jonathan Baumbach	7.95	3.95
Things in Place by Jerry Bumpus	8.95	3.95
Ø Null Set by George Chambers	8.95	3.95
The Winnebago Mysteries by Moira Crone	10.95	4.95
Amateur People by Andrée Connors	8.95	3.95
Take It or Leave It by Raymond Federman	11.95	4.95
Coming Close by B.H. Friedman	11.95	5.95
Museum by B.H. Friedman	7.95	3.95
Temporary Sanity by Thomas Glynn	8.95	3.95
The Talking Room by Marianne Hauser	8.95	3.95
Holy Smoke by Fanny Howe	8.95	3.95
Mole's Pity by Harold Jaffe	8.95	3.95
Mourning Crazy Horse by Harold Jaffe	11.95	5.95
Moving Parts by Steve Katz	8.95	3.95
Find Him! by Elaine Kraf	9.95	3.95
I Smell Esther Williams by Mark Leyner	11.95	5.95
Emergency Exit by Clarence Major	9.95	4.95
Reflex and Bone Structure by Clarence Major	8.95	3.95
Four Roses in Three Acts by Franklin Mason	9.95	4.95
The Secret Table by Mark Mirsky	7.95	3.95
Encores for a Dilettante by Ursule Molinaro	8.95	3.95
Rope Dances by David Porush	8.95	3.95
The Broad Back of the Angel by Leon Rooke	9.95	3.95
The Common Wilderness by Michael Seide	16.95	——
The Comatose Kids by Seymour Simckes	8.95	3.95
Fat People by Carol Sturm Smith	8.95	3.95
The Hermetic Whore by Peter Spielberg	8.95	3.95
Twiddledum Twaddledum by Peter Spielberg	7.95	3.95
Long Talking Bad Conditions Blues by Ronald Sukenick	9.95	4.95
98.6 by Ronald Sukenick	7.95	3.95
Meningitis by Yuriy Tarnawsky	8.95	3.95
Heretical Songs by Curtis White	9.95	4.95
Statements 1	——	3.95
Statements 2	8.95	2.95

Order from Flatiron Book Distributors Inc., 175 Fifth Avenue (Suite 814), NYC 10010